WILLOW BASIN

OTHER FIVE STAR WESTERNS BY PETER DAWSON:

Dark Riders of Doom (1996)
Rattlesnake Mesa (1997)
Ghost Brand of the Wishbones (1998)
Angel Peak (1999)
Claiming of the Deerfoot (2000)
Lone Rider from Texas (2001)
Forgotten Destiny (2002)
Phantom Raiders (2003)
Ghost of the Chinook (2004)
Showdown at Anchor (2005)
Desert Drive (2006)
Troublesome Range (2007)
Posse Guns (2008)
Gunsmoke Masquerade (2009)

Willow Basin

A Western Sextet

Peter Dawson

FIVE STAR
A part of Gale, Cengage Learning

Detroit • New York • San Francisco • New Haven, Conn • Waterville, Maine • London

Five Star Publishing, a part of Gale, Cengage Learning.

Set in 11 pt. Plantin.

LIBRARY OF CONGRESS CATALOGING-IN-PUBLICATION DATA

Dawson, Peter, 1907–1957.
Willow Basin : a western sextet / by Peter Dawson. — 1st ed.
p. cm.
ISBN-13: 978-1-59414-900-9 (hardcover)
ISBN-10: 1-59414-900-3 (hardcover)
1. Western stories. I. Title.
PS3507.A848W56 2010
813′.52—dc22 2010013264

First Edition. First Printing: August 2010.
Published in 2010 in conjunction with Golden West Literary Agency.

Printed in the United States of America
1 2 3 4 5 6 7 14 13 12 11 10

CONTENTS

POSSE OF OUTLAWED MEN 7

RUST OFF A TIN STAR 45

NESTER PAYOFF 77

AMATEUR GUN GUARD 99

DEAD MAN'S ASSAY 127

WILLOW BASIN 181

★ ★ ★ ★ ★

Posse of Outlawed Men

★ ★ ★ ★ ★

Jon Glidden's title for this story was "Six of Gun-Jacks". It was the fifth story he had written and it was submitted by his agent to *Big-Book Western* in July, 1936. It was accepted on January 11, 1937 and the author was paid $90. Upon publication the title was changed to "Posse of Outlawed Men" in the issue dated March-April, 1937. For its appearance here the magazine's title has been retained.

I

An air of tense expectancy ran through the crowd that milled in the dusty street before the courthouse of Singletree. It was the appearance of a black-garbed figure in the doorway of the building that abruptly quieted the undertone of conversation. All eyes turned upward to watch the man as he came to the head of the steps, flanked by four sober-faced, gun-belted men. His glance shuttled briefly over the throng below before he sauntered down, seemingly unaware of the presence of these watchers.

He made an impressive figure even though he was shorter than the average in this country of tall men; for in his swaggering walk, the outthrust chin, and in the gray eyes that were hard as polished granite, there was a suggestion of rugged strength that made up for his lack of height. At the foot of the steps the crowd gave way and the little knot of men passed through and across the street. Covertly hostile glances followed them, but it was obvious that the man and his bodyguards commanded a belligerent respect.

Ahead of him, one of his guards turned in from the awninged walk to shoulder through the slatted doors of a saloon. Inside, the gunman stopped in mid-stride, his right hand falling smoothly to the butt of the Colt, tied low on his thigh.

"Easy, Ace!" ordered the man in black to his guard as he pushed into the saloon a moment later, and at the command the guard's poised hand dropped away from the gun butt.

The man in black squinted a little, searching through the half light of the room until he saw the lone man who stood quietly regarding him from the center of the bar to his left. There were others there, too, but they stood across the room and he ignored them.

"I thought I told you to leave Singletree, Montana," he said.

The shadow of a smile played across the angular features of the man called Montana. His brown eyes glinted with some inner amusement, and then the look hardened as his face went expressionless. "I don't scare easy, Frazer," he answered levelly, shifting his back-thrust elbows a little on the bar top. "Thought I'd hang around and see you finish the framing."

Frazer flushed at the words. "You're makin' big talk," he rasped, spacing his words carefully to hide his annoyance. The hard lines of his thin-lipped face made him ugly as he edged forward a little to give the others behind him room to enter.

"Nothing I'm saying that I won't back up," Montana drawled tauntingly. "Any time."

Effortlessly Montana pushed himself erect from his slouch against the bar. His tall, flat-hipped frame was deceptively relaxed as he stood there, calmly surveying the five men at the door. From the crown of his soiled Stetson to the toes of his soft high-heeled boots he was quietly alert.

Behind Frazer there was the hint of a stealthy movement. At this instant Montana lunged sideways, his hand sweeping downward and rising in a blasting stab of flame. The man behind Frazer spun about, crashing into the wall, and a choked cry broke from his twisted lips. The Colt he had been swinging upward pounded solidly to the floor and a splotch of crimson spread across his right shoulder. The others stood unmoving, tense and watchful, ignoring the wounded man's muttered oaths.

The smoke curled upward from the blue snout of his Colt as Montana straightened and once more took his position at the bar. He flicked the .45 back into his worn holster. "Anybody else want more of that medicine?" he asked in quiet defiance.

For seconds the air was heavy with pending action; the silence was like that interval between a lightning flash and the ensuing thunder. It was a silence that branded these five men at the door as nerveless, standing as they were before the deadly swiftness of this drawling cowpuncher.

A shout from the outside broke the tension. Through the doors slammed a tall, shad-bellied oldster wearing a sheriff's badge. He stood glaring about, his black-browed gaze fixed for an instant on the wounded man who still leaned against the wall, then abruptly he singled out Montana.

"What the hell's this?" he boomed, standing with feet spread a little, and pushing his hat onto the back of his of his hairless head.

"You missed it, Sheriff," Montana told him. "This sidewinder. . . ."

"Arrest him, Canby!" Frazer cut in.

The sheriff looked first at Montana, then at Frazer, and finally back again to Montana. "You're under arrest, Pierce," the lawman echoed in compliance with orders of the man in black. "I'm damned I'll let any gunslinger raise this kind of hell in Singletree."

Montana calmly surveyed the sheriff. Finally he spoke, stopping Canby's move to come forward. "Frazer, why don't you get the rest of your outfit? Send out for Judge Solon, some more of your Bar Z hairpins, and your open-range homesteaders that sat in the jury today. So they convicted Clem Walker. You framed him and made it stick. Maybe with enough men backing you, you'd make this new stunt of yours stick. As it is, you're plumb harmless."

"Pierce, you're under arrest," Canby repeated, but now his tones had none of the certainty they had had a moment before.

"Hand over your hardware."

Montana's wary glance shuttled over to Frazer and his men, finally coming back to Canby. "And here we have a lawman," he sneered in mocking derision. "Canby, if you come one step closer, I'll blow you hell to breakfast."

He leaned forward a little, and again there was that flip of his hand that brought his Colt hip high, covering the men before him before they could move. He sidled away from the bar, circling toward an open window that let out onto the street, moving with a cat-like ease. Frazer and his men pivoted as he moved, following him with their eyes.

When he stood at the window, he said: "There's six of you standing there. Why doesn't someone make a play? Canby, next time you try to make an arrest have someone along who'll back your play."

Montana stepped through the window. Frazer let out an oath and turned toward the doors, pushing his men ahead of him. Canby crowded behind, drawing his two .45s. Outside, the Bar Z gunnies came to an abrupt halt. Montana had waited beside the window and now held the steady muzzle of his Colt lined at the group.

"You gents stay set," he told them. "I'm up this alley. The first ranny who follows me gets cut to doll rags."

Lazily he stepped backward, a tight smile of reckless challenge on his lips. Abruptly he was gone.

Frazer cursed his men, but not one of them attempted to follow. Canby finally pushed through and started for the alley, broke into a run when the pounding of hoofs echoed between the buildings. When he turned into the alley, it was empty.

Across the street on the courthouse steps, stood two people who had witnessed what had gone on in the street. One of them was a girl of perhaps twenty whose quizzical hazel-eyed glance traveled on up to the end of the street where a rider suddenly had appeared from between two adobe houses.

"There he goes, Jim," she said, speaking to the man who stood beside her. "What does it mean?"

"Mean?" he echoed, his wrinkled face lined with a frown. "Nothin'."

"That was Montana Pierce, Jim."

"Uhn-huh. He quit workin' for Frazer the day your dad was arrested."

"He had a gun on Canby and Frazer," she said, puzzlement written on her ivory-tinted face. "That's queer,"

"What's queer about it?" Jim asked. "Those trigger wizards are always havin' scrapes. Montana's just another Bar Z polecat, Miss Betty."

She was silent a moment, looking across the street to where the crowd milled about the saloon entrance. "Perhaps he's broken with Frazer after this. Any decent man would."

Jim snorted. "Miss Betty, you're forgettin' that it was men like Montana and Frazer that put your dad behind the bars."

Betty shook her head. "But he's different," she insisted. "I don't believe Montana took any part in what they did to Dad."

"Don't let him fool you," Jim told her. "He's just another no account gunslingin' saddle bum or he wouldn't have hired out to Frazer in the first place. He probably helped Frazer plant that stolen herd in our pasture."

"You don't know it was Frazer," she flared. "How can you be so sure?"

"Common sense," Jim reasoned. "Who else would want to get Clem Walker out of the way? Who's hoggin' the range and drivin' the little fellow off? It couldn't be anyone but Frazer. He's after the Circle W water and he'll get it one way or another. And just because we're strangers here . . . because only three years on this range still makes us strangers . . . these gutless people are goin' to stand by and let him do it."

"There must be enough decent people around to stop a thing like this."

"There aren't," Jim asserted explosively. "The trial today showed they're lily-livered when it comes to buckin' the Bar Z. It was one of Frazer's hands who found the rustled stock in our pasture and reported it to Canby. It was a parcel of Frazer's open-range homesteaders on the jury today that found your dad guilty. The idea of Clem Walker bein' convicted on a rustlin' charge may seem addle-headed to us because we know him, but he's still a stranger in this country. Frazer framed Clem Walker, had him tried, and is makin' it stick."

"Let's ride, Jim." Betty sighed. "I've got to get out of here."

II

They went out into the street, followed by curious glances of those about them, got their horses at the livery stable, and headed out of town. They rode out across the bench-like grasslands that stretched away toward the low hazy foothills. It was midafternoon and the sun's glare made the shimmering distance deceptive so that the jagged peaks of the Antelopes seemed far off and floating in an ocean of blue fog.

"What's next?" Betty Walker finally asked in a small voice. "Will you be looking for another job, Jim?"

Jim jerked a sideward glance at her and half turned in the saddle. "Do you think I'm leavin' after sidin' Clem for the last ten years?" His glance softened as he took in Betty's drooping figure. "We'll get through this some way. Don't you fret about that."

Betty was silent, half-heartedly glad that things were finally settled. The last few days had been slow torture for her. Clem Walker's arrest had come without warning, and the three days since he entered jail had been spent in a frantic, useless search for evidence that would prove his innocence. Now it was over and to be in the saddle once again and riding through the stillness of this vast open range was a relief, yet it left her feeling alone and weary. Jim, for the first time, now saw the worry that Betty had so well concealed for the past few days, written plainly on her fine-featured face.

"We'll go along without Clem for a spell, Miss Betty," Jim said. "Give me a little time and I'll hunt down the coyotes that planted that wet beef on us. It won't be long before your dad's back again."

The shadow of some inner thought took the light out of her eyes. "Jim, I haven't told you, but we're in bad shape." Her face was averted, and he could not read the expression on it.

"Bad shape?" he echoed. "Oh, well, we'll make out."

"Not if the herds keep falling off," she insisted. "We aren't going to have much of a count this roundup."

"We'll see they don't fall off any more."

"How can we? We haven't the money to hire the men it would take to guard them. No, Jim, unless we can get Dad back to run things, we'll be cleaned out before another year rolls around."

Suddenly realizing that she was right, Jim made no attempt to deny the fact. This thing had been uppermost in his mind even before the calamity of Clem's arrest struck them. The fire went out of him and he slouched in the saddle, his spare figure drooping with an utter weariness. "Somethin' may happen to help," he said lamely and without conviction.

A heavy silence hung over them for the rest of their ten-mile ride. Long before the weathered frame buildings of the Circle W rose up out of the distance, the sky had banked with black thunderclouds seeming to suit their mood. The breeze that had been gently stirring across the distances gave way to a sultry stillness and the heat became oppressive. The sun, red for the past hour, finally lost itself in a haze that rose up out of the distant mountain valleys.

"The arroyos'll be runnin' water before sundown," Jim said. Betty made no answer, and he could not be sure that she had heard.

The storm began in a low muttering of far-off thunder, shortly before the too early darkness blanketed down over the plain. For an hour a hushed stillness deadened all the evening sounds, then the rain started slowly at first, coming down in huge splashing drops until it gathered in volume to a pelting downpour.

Under the protection of the wide porch that ran across the face of the bunkhouse, Jim and two others sat in the darkness, watching the storm. The two, along with two more riders who were now at a line camp in the hills, completed the Circle W crew that had formerly numbered a dozen riders.

Clem Walker had let his men go one by one as the spread drifted toward certain financial ruin. Rustling had taken a heavy toll on the herds, and Walker, powerless to keep them guarded in the face of a constant danger, had seen the Circle W sapped of its strength. Now, no longer drawing pay, the four men besides Jim were staying on out of sheer loyalty to a man they had learned to respect deeply.

The three on the bunkhouse porch were wordless, watching the ferocity of the storm in complete silence. Sharp rolling bursts of thunder punctuated the lightning flashes that showed the drenched landscape in the distance. The steady drone of the downpour filled in the intervals between the lightning crashes.

The road that led away from the yard was running water that had already cut deep gashes in the loose, rutted soil. In the brief glimpses they had of it they could follow the course of the torrent until it dropped into an arroyo at the foot of the slope.

In one of those split-second flashes they saw a rider outlined against the grayness beyond, coming up the road, his horse at a walk. Jim got up out of his chair, waited impatiently for the few

seconds until there was another lightning flash and he could see the man again.

"Get your irons," he ordered finally, and the other two faded through the inky shadow of the doorway. When he turned, he told them: "He's headin' for the house. Rick, you go over and get in the back way. Don't show a light until you savvy what this is all about. Al and I will go out front and meet him. It may not mean trouble, but there's a lot of two-legged coyotes runnin' loose on this range. We can't take chances with Miss Betty here."

None of them took the time to get their ponchos, but, dressed as they were, they ran out into the storm and across to the house. Jim and Al had waited less than ten seconds when there was a call from out front.

"Hello!"

"Hello, yourself!" Jim answered. "Who is it?"

"Montana Pierce!"

Montana sat hunched over in the saddle, his face shielded against the driving rain by the rim of his Stetson, waiting for the voice he had recognized as Jim Early's to reply. He was about to shout out his name again, thinking he had not been heard, when Jim finally spoke gruffly out of the blackness of the porch: "Light and come on in!"

Montana swung stiffly to the ground, unbuckled his poncho, and threw it over his saddle. "Hell of a night!" he said as he stepped in under the wide porch roof.

"What'll you have?" Jim asked in unwelcoming abruptness.

"I rode out to see Miss Walker."

"Maybe she don't want to see you," came Jim's blunt statement. "Frazer's gunnies aren't welcome here."

A rectangle of light all at once flooded out onto the porch as the house door swung open. Framed in the light was Betty Walker's straight, delicately rounded figure.

"Jim," she said, "any man's welcome in this storm. Come in, Montana."

Montana followed her into the house, feeling a little awkward in her presence, wondering if he should have chosen this way of helping her. His eyes followed her every move, tasting the peculiar thrill it gave him to be this close to her. Betty Walker affected him that way—strangely, too, for Montana was unwilling to admit to himself even yet, that any woman could interest him. She seemed more real than other girls he had known, for there was no pretense about her. When she spoke, her mellow tones carried a conviction that was heightened by the directness of the look in her hazel eyes.

Montana had never thought of her as being beautiful, yet instinctively he knew that she was. Her perfectly formed features were set in a strong, though delicately feminine face that was expressive of her every mood. There was a poise about her that showed strength and character. Even now, knowing that she must be wearied to the core over the events of the day, he saw that her boyishly square shoulders were back, her carriage erect, and her chin set in clear indication she was not beaten.

"You've a lot of explainin' to do, Montana," Jim spoke up. "Let's have it."

"I heard you needed a man out here," Montana said, speaking to Betty. "I came out for the job."

"We told no one we needed a man," she answered him, a puzzled frown wrinkling her high forehead.

"I reckon you didn't," he admitted. "But you'll be needing help now with your dad gone."

"We're lookin' out for ourselves." Jim's voice boomed. "We don't have any use for gunslingers."

"I can rope and ride better'n any man on this spread," Montana told Jim levelly.

"Get this, Montana," Jim began, "we. . . ."

"But it's true, Jim," Betty cut in. "We need men . . . any men who'll take our starvation wages."

Jim turned somber eyes on her. "I've worked for Clem Walker the best part of my life and we've never had to hire jacks to keep our own. It's too late to start now. If you want to take Pierce on, you don't want me." His glance swung around to rake Montana.

"I reckon I'll go," Montana answered levelly. "I only wanted to help."

Jim said: "If you want to help, then ride out of here."

Montana smiled meagerly, shrugged, and turned away. He might have expected this. Deep within him he knew that Jim belonged here—that it was no choice Betty could make. If the Circle W was to go down, it would go down Clem Walker's way—string-straight and fine.

He crossed the porch and walked out through the driving downpour to where his thick-shouldered chestnut gelding stood with down-hanging head. His movements were mechanical as he threw on his poncho, climbed to the saddle, and rode away. This way, then, was closed.

Once before he had seen men make their own law, as Frazer was doing. That time five forked men had driven him out of the Coconiño Sink—had driven him to killing two of them. It was a hard lesson, but he had learned it. If it had worked once for them, it would work again, this time for him.

So, two days afterward, he faced five more men. But this time the five men were listening to him. It was in a shack far up Bitter Creek Cañon. He had chosen well. Each man here hated Frazer, had been robbed, broken, beaten by him.

Of them all, Peewee Steele was the biggest and the most stubborn. His thoughtful face and his unhurried manner would be indicative of the thoughts of the rest. The time it took him to come to a decision would give Gabe Halpin time to cool off,

Rand Avery time to recall the gun-whipping Ace Doolin had given him, and Ben Tilton time to let his old man's grudge freshen. Juan Mercado needed no urging, for two years he had been waiting for the chance to avenge Frazer's desertion of his sister.

His face unsmiling, his voice level, he had told them of his plan. He was completing his instructions to Peewee: ". . . So you see, you'll risk your neck, Peewee, but if it fails, you'll ride out of the country with the rest of us . . . ride hard, hell for leather."

Gabe Halpin's long frame seemed to couple together as he lounged from the table, faced Peewee, and said softly: "That don't take thinking out, Peewee."

Juan Mercado said: "Me, I'm theenk Frazer look more better weeth knife in his neck."

"Some rannies would rather die that way than lose land," Ben Tilton said. "Frazer's one of 'em."

Rand Avery said, stroking a scar on his cheek: "We're only six, but what the hell. I'll chance it."

"The two Wheeler boys are in it. I came from their layout this afternoon," Montana said. He had been saving this as a driving wedge.

Now they tangled. Ben Tilton was dubious, impervious to Gabe Halpin's scorn; Mercado had a different plan. Avery was quiet, watching Peewee. Finally Montana said: "How about it, Pewee?"

Pewee looked carefully at his fingernails and said slowly, softly: "Let's try it your way, Montana. If anything'll ever work, it will."

Montana's glance shuttled over these men. He said: "Do you all want it my way?" When they nodded, his face relaxed for the first time. "Wheeler's spread is closest to the railroad. We can push 'em from Gabe's Rocking H. . . ."

"Not mine any more," Gabe cut in bitterly. "Not since Frazer burned me out."

Montana corrected himself. "We can push 'em from what used to be Gabe's place, over the *malpaís*"—he allowed himself a down-bearing smile—"you rustlers."

III

Shortly before daybreak Montana sat hunkered down, his back against a jack pine, scanning carefully a pasture that was bordered by the stand of timber in which he was hiding. In the ghostly light of the moon he could pick out the darker shadows that he knew were cattle. Here was the Bar Z pasture where Henry Crossan rode herd, and, if he was not mistaken, it was Henry Crossan who was slowly circling the herd and heading toward him. It seemed an eternity before the rider came close enough for Montana to recognize him, yet, when he saw the black and white checked shirt, he knew that he had found his man. He hailed him softly, and, as the sound of his voice drifted out across the still air, Crossan shifted suddenly in the saddle and his hand dipped to draw the carbine from the scabbard on the far side of his horse. He did not move for several seconds but then advanced slowly toward Montana, his Winchester ready in the crook of his arm.

"What d' you want?" he growled when he was still twenty yards away.

"Howdy, Henry."

Crossan gave a visible start. "Well, I'll . . . !" The rest of his words were lost as he spurred forward and drew rein a short distance away. "Come out and show yourself!"

Montana came out into the light. "Did you think I'd skipped the country?" he asked.

"Hell, no," Henry replied. "Not you."

"Henry, we're out to cut in on Frazer's play," Montana told

him, coming abruptly to the purpose of his visit. "Peewee, Gabe, Halpin, the Wheeler boys, and a few others. Want to come in on it?"

In the strong light of the moon, Montana caught Henry's startled look, saw the broad grin that spread across his lean face. "Do I want in on it?" he exclaimed. "Am I loco? Sure, I'm in."

Montana was silent a moment, then said: "I've been figurin', Henry. You're using the Bar Z as a hide-out from something or other, or you wouldn't stay two minutes riding herd for a sidewinder like Frazer."

Crossan gave him a long look before he replied. "Seems like more'n one of Frazer's hairpins is on the dodge. I don't deny it."

"Doesn't mean a thing to me." Montana shrugged. "Only I wanted to get it straight. I've heard you speak your mind once or twice about Frazer. I figure you're aching to see him pay for a few of the things he's done. Well, so are the rest of us."

"Montana, if there's anything I can do to help you put that polecat at the end of a rope, I'm with you. When do we ride?"

Montana quickly ran over in his mind the things he knew about Crossan: his straightforwardness, his sincere loathing of Frazer's methods, and lastly that queer unspoken friendship that he had for the man. If he was any judge at all, Crossan would fit in with his plans.

"You're good to me right where you are," Montana said to him. "There's enough in our bunch to handle things on the outside. If you'll stay at the Bar Z and work from the inside, you'll be doing the most good."

"What do I do?"

"Nothing yet. In a day or so I'll be back. You'll be here?"

"I reckon," Henry replied. "I've been here three weeks now, and Frazer ain't goin' to take the guards off his critters."

They talked a few minutes more and then Montana left, satisfied that Henry fitted in with the plans. An hour later he was four miles back in the hills where he made a fireless camp. As he lay in the blankets, looking up at the winking stars he felt a strange elation. In planning all this he had not realized how willingly others would join him. Finally he closed his eyes, anxious that sleep should bring closer his meeting with Peewee and the rest.

A rope snaked down from above to coil half its length on a rocky ledge sixty feet above the cañon floor. As it etched its thin line against the star-sprinkled void of the sky, six dark, silent figures came down it hand over hand to stand on the ledge.

Montana waited until Gabe stood beside him. "Which way?" he asked.

In answer, Gabe moved off to his right and they started down through the tumbled mass of rock and stunted piñon. Once Montana cautioned Gabe about going too fast, as Peewee loosed a small rock from above. Luckily it did not roll far, but from there on they proceeded with more caution.

Below, Montana could see the outlines of the three buildings, one larger than the others. This larger building was in the center of a barren plot of ground. Forty feet behind it, almost directly underneath their path, was a fringe of tall cedars. Darkness hid the cattle that Montana knew were grazing in the pasture that ran down the center of the wide cañon.

When they were in the trees below behind the house, Montana sent Juan off first, giving him a five minute start before the others melted into the shadows after him. He stood with Gabe a moment, watching Peewee's bulk disappear through the trees. Then he stepped out, walked silently across the open stretch of ground to the rear of the main building. Quickly he crawled beneath an open window along the side wall and drew up at the front corner.

It took him ten long seconds to creep into the shadows of the unfloored porch, Gabe following closely behind. They waited a moment beside the open door, and then Montana abruptly stepped inside, drawing his Colt. The silence of his entrance was unbroken for long moments. Then Gabe stepped in after him and there was an ominous creaking of a loose board. The low snoring of a man in a bunk at the right continued unbroken, but at once Montana heard a stealthy movement across the room.

"Who the hell's that?" came a voice the next instant. There was a short, tense silence. Then: "Wake up, boys! There's someone in here!"

Montana waited, heard the others stir. Across the room he heard a man climb from his bunk and move stealthily along the far wall.

Crash!

A thundering shot unexpectedly blasted the silence. Montana instinctively swung his Colt around, thumbed a shot at the floor in the direction of the gun flash. "Throw down your cutters!" he called out sharply. "We've got the place surrounded!"

"Like hell!" came an angry snarl, punctuated with the crashing roar of a .45 that momentarily lighted the room with its purple flame stab. Gabe's Colt tore loose in an instantaneous answer. It was followed by a choked groan, and after a moment the dull thud of a body falling.

"Someone light the lamp," came another voice. "Bill's hurt bad."

"Don't be a damn' fool!" barked another. "There's two of 'em waitin' to cut down on us."

Montana groped about him, found Gabe, and pulled him by the sleeve along the wall and into a corner. Some instinct must have prompted him to change his position for the next instant three .45s launched staccato blast from the other end of the room.

The beating inferno of those shots had not yet died down when there came a crash as a table overturned, and the men opposite rushed to the spot where Gabe and Montana had been. Montana saw one of the figures framed in the paler light of the doorway. He swung his Colt around, felt it buck in his hand, then threw himself to the floor.

As two .45s cut loose at the spot where he had stood, he saw the figure in the doorway stumble backward and fall out onto the porch. From outside came the muffled sound of two closely spaced shots. There a momentary silence before three more shots thudded out. In the room no one moved. Montana waited.

"Let's cut loose of this place," came a loud whisper. "There's more outside."

Without stopping to answer, figures plunged through the doorway. Montana and Gabe thumbed their .45s, spattering the floor near the door with their slugs, aiming low. The three gained the porch, only to be brought up short as Ben Tilton's voice boomed out of the darkness: "Stand where you are, gents!"

Montana was on his feet, and in two strides was standing at the door. "Reach," he drawled quietly. "You're through."

In the dim light he saw the three hesitate one brief instant. He fired once, could see where the bullet kicked up dust at their feet. At that, they dropped their six-guns, slowly raised their hands.

Montana and Gabe picked up their guns. Searching the men, Montana found two knives and a small, wicked-looking Derringer. As he stepped away and called to Ben, Peewee and Rand Avery rounded the back corner of the building, prodding before them two other prisoners.

"There's one ranny out there who won't ever straddle his hull again," Pewee announced.

"Ben, you and Gabe hightail down and help Juan with that guard," Montana said quickly. "If he's had any trouble. . . ."

"No one 'ave trouble, Montana," came a voice close at hand. Juan came up out of the shadows. "The *hombre* up there keeck up wan beeg fuss. It was hees last."

"Take a look over here!" Peewee called out now, from around the corner of the building. Montana walked over, saw him bending over a prone figure on the ground. "Look what was trying to crawl away."

Montana looked more closely, and even in the dim light recognized the thin hawk-like features of Peewee's captive.

"Howdy, Ace," Montana said levelly, trying to keep the surprise out of his voice. "So you're running this end of Frazer's business?"

"Pierce, your carcass won't be worth a spick *peso* when Frazer hears about this."

"Ace, you were along the other day in Singletree when I told Frazer I couldn't be scared out. I haven't changed my mind." He paused, but Ace made no answer, so he went on. "Peewee, look Ace over and patch him up. He's leading his gunnies home."

In ten minutes, five Bar Z horses stood with their riders lashed face down across their saddles, hands and feet laced together under the horses' bellies. Ace Doolin, the Bar Z ramrod, was astride his saddle with his feet bound tightly to the cinch.

Montana took Ben aside. "Take 'em as far as the alfalfa this side of the breaks. Turn 'em loose and hightail over to Wheelers'. We'll meet you there sometime tomorrow."

"Montana," came Ace's voice, "loosen this damned rope. That spick's got me tied tighter'n a fence wire."

"I reckon you'll make it home all right, Ace," Montana answered. "Tell Frazer we went easy on you rannies tonight. Next time, it'll be different."

"You figure Frazer'll let this go by without huntin' you down?" Ace snarled.

"I've quit tryin' to figure him," Montana answered. "But I'm makin' this stick. Now get going."

IV

The faint, gray flush of dawn showed in the east when Ace Doolin's paint gelding plodded patiently into the large corral that stood below the ranch house of the Bar Z. Ace was slumped forward in the saddle, his head hanging weakly above the gelding's withers. Two other jaw-branded Bar Z horses loomed up out of the shadows to stand beside Ace's horse, the unwieldy bulk of the riders lashed across the saddles making the animals misshapen in the half light.

"Ace," came the choked cry from one of the bound gunnies. "Ace, damn it, wake up. Get me off this jughead."

Ace stirred visibly, came slowly back to consciousness, realizing that the animal he rode was standing motionlessly. He raised his head, looked vacantly about him for a moment, and gradually picked out familiar objects until there came a full understanding that this nightmare was nearly over.

He was weak from the loss of blood, but the chill of the crisp air acted as a tonic to clear his befuddled senses. He shouted once, tried to knee his gelding around the corral and up to the house, but the stubborn animal would not respond, so he continued his hoarse croaking until a light appeared in the bunkhouse window and the dark figures of men came running.

When they had unlashed him and lifted him from the saddle, he said: "A couple of you rannies head out toward the breaks and pick up the other three. Slippery's bronc' was buckin' like hell, tryin' to shake Slippery off. The other two followed him."

They carried Ace up to the house, meeting Frazer on the way. The two other riders were taken to the bunkhouse, given a drink of whiskey, and put to bed.

Frazer had Ace carried into his office, a small room at the front corner of the large frame building. He hurriedly lit the lamp, watching while one of the men ripped Ace's shirt away and bandaged his wound.

"Who did this?" Frazer asked.

"Montana Pierce," Ace growled. "He's raided the place up at Bitter Creek, beefed Bill Rowan, and shot up Frank Humphreys and Pete Crowe. Outside of that, he's drivin' off the herd. There were eight or ten of them, maybe a dozen. We didn't have a chance."

"Why didn't Scotty signal you they were comin'?" Frazer asked. "Wasn't he posted at the Narrows?"

"Sure," Ace drawled sarcastically. "Sure, but they got to 'im. Juan Mercado took care of him."

"Is that knifin' spick sidin' Montana?"

"He is"—Ace nodded—"along with some other salty rannies. Gabe Halpin, Peewee Steele, Ben Tilton, and a few others. Just a pack of your friends, boss."

Frazer paced nervously up and down in front of Ace's chair, his heels clicking on the bare floorboards.

"Well," Ace said finally, "are you goin' to stay here and let him drive off all that rustled beef?"

Frazer stared thoughtfully before him for a long moment. The dull yellow glow of the lamp on the desk served to accentuate the breadth of his chunky figure and threw along the wall an enlarged, ape-like shadow that was strangely weird.

"This is somethin' that calls for thought and not powder smoke, Ace. We'll let Pierce get away with it this once. Maybe next time he'll make a mistake cuttin' in on my game. If he does . . . we'll see," he said ominously.

Ten days later, in midafternoon, Montana was riding across the northern edge of Circle W range, half a mile out from the foothills, heading toward that spur of timber that bordered the Bar Z pasture where Henry Crossan rode herd. The events of the past few days had wrought a subtle change in him. His lean, angular face was lined with an unnatural frown that came from an intense inner weariness, for there had been hard riding and little sleep since the raid on Gabe Halpin's old spread.

But there was satisfaction in thinking of what he had accomplished. After the raid in Bitter Creek Cañon, they had driven out of it three hundred head of cattle that showed signs of recent branding. They had spent all the next day driving them through the hills and across the mountains by way of a low pass. Late the same night they had arrived at the Rafter W hill pasture and left the herd in charge of the Wheeler brothers. The next night they had driven off Frazer's herd of fine yearlings from his western-most range, far distant from the Bar Z. As before, the two gunnies who guarded the herd had been lashed to their saddles and taken back to the Bar Z by Ben Tilton.

Then came the most daring threat to Frazer's strength—the raid on Halfway Wells. The wells supplied water to four thousand acres of open range on which Frazer had recently planted his homesteaders. Montana's men swooped down on the camp, dynamited the wells, and rode off leaving the dull orange of burning buildings lighting up the heavens.

Frazer called in Sheriff Canby then, and for four days now Montana and his men had watched from afar the aimless wanderings of a posse of Bar Z riders, headed by Canby. Although they had been safe the whole time, there was a constant strain.

Frazer's strength was ebbing, his herds diminishing in the same way as had those of the neighboring ranches on which Bar Z had secretly preyed for so long. His range around Halfway Wells was useless without water, and the herds that dotted it were already moving out.

Montana's thoughts were interrupted as he sighted a rider coming toward him, still a speck ahead on the brown and green pattern of the level prairie. The sight of the rider pulled him to an abrupt stop while he debated whether or not to ride the half mile north to the safety of the foothills. His eyes, accustomed to distances, studied the bay horse and found about its swinging run something familiar. Unconsciously he thumbed out the butt of his Colt, deciding to ride on and meet the oncoming horseman. Then came an abrupt recognition of who this was. Betty Walker.

The bay came up fast, leaving behind a plume of dust spreading out in the hot air. A surge of excitement hit Montana and he found himself welcoming this meeting. He noted the lithe grace with which Betty sat the saddle, the rhythm of her slender figure seeming to blend in with the powerful strides of the animal she rode. She wore blue Levi's and a tan shirt. As she slid the bay to a stop in front of him, her hair took on the burnished gold of the sunlight.

"Howdy, Miss Walker," he greeted, touching the brim of his hat.

She did not answer immediately, but sat eyeing him with a half quizzical, unsmiling expression. Abruptly she asked: "Why are you doing it, Montana?"

The directness of the question startled him, and, while he was groping for an answer, she went on.

"I never thought you'd go this way."

"What way?" he asked.

"To take to the owlhoot. With a price on your head."

He smiled. "That's something new. The reward, I mean."

"Frazer's offered fifteen hundred dollars for your capture, dead or alive," she told him, her unflinching gaze boldly meeting his.

"Maybe I ought to offer a reward for him," Montana said easily. "We're two of a kind."

"You are not," she flared. "In a week since I saw you, you've done more harm than Frazer ever did on this range."

"Harm?" He shrugged. "I reckon Frazer's the only one who has a complaint to make."

"What about Halfway Wells?" she asked him. "Four thousand acres left without water. There were seven small ranches on that land. You ruined them."

"They were Frazer's," he said firmly. "Frazer hired those homesteaders, planted them on what was open range two years ago. In another year he'd have gone through the pretense of buying 'em out. It was his scheme to hog more land and drive off the other outfits."

For a moment she looked at him with a certain defiance. "You're being selfish, Montana. You and the rest that ride with you are settling a grudge. What you're doing won't help the rest of us."

"Why should I help?" he queried, laughing scornfully. "Neither you nor any of the rest would trust me. You wouldn't even give me a job."

"It wasn't I who turned you away," she said levelly. "It was Jim."

"Then you . . . ," Montana began, but caught himself.

"I've never believed what they said of you," came her soft-spoken words. "I still don't. You aren't a killer, Montana."

He sat silently, at first unbelieving. Slowly her words took root in his mind and with startling clarity he saw that she believed in him, that she was sincere. Then it was that he understood how blindly he had gone about his selfish mission of vengeance, and that his real wish all along had been to right the wrong done to Clem Walker and his daughter. He had struck at Frazer, not thinking that others besides himself and his men had a grievance against the man. Her words cut in on his thoughts.

"He'll turn all these things against you. You'll be hunted by every rancher around Singletree. If you really want to help, as you say, get some proof against Frazer. But don't keep on with this awful burning, stealing, killing. . . ." A half sob choked off her words as she wheeled the bay around and abruptly rode away.

He watched her until she disappeared behind a low ridge in the distance. Only then did he continue on the trail that would take him to Henry Crossan. It was with a wild surge of elation that he realized how Betty's words had crystallized his blind thrusts at the Bar Z owner into one definite purpose. And then came the knowledge that she cared.

A seed of a plan grew in his mind, shaped itself into something so daring as to be incredible. He rode onward, twisting the reins over the saddle horn and building a cigarette. And to the accompaniment of the creak of saddle leather and the hollow ring of his gelding's hoofs on the bare rock, he weighed the chances of his seeing this new plan through.

V

Two hours after sundown that evening, Ralph Frazer and Ace Doolin sat in the small office of the Bar Z. Frazer occupied the chair behind the desk, facing the outside door, while Ace sat tilted back against the outside wall. Ace was softly cursing his clumsiness at rolling a cigarette, for his right arm was still stiff from the wound Montana had given him.

The Bar Z owner's black brows contracted in a frown.

"What's eatin' you, Ace?" he asked.

Ace looked up then, seeming to measure Frazer with his glance. "You're goin' soft, boss," came his startling statement.

"Why don't you let me gather up the boys and ride out after that coyote?"

Frazer chuckled. "If you held four aces, would you bet the limit and get the counter-jumpers out of the game?"

"No," Ace answered, after due deliberation. "I reckon I'd play 'em close and keep the others in for a grand killin'. But I can't see that you're holding four aces this hand, boss."

"I'm not . . . yet! But after Pierce cuts loose a few more times, I will be. I'm lettin' him build himself a reputation, Ace. When he has one, there won't be a rancher in these parts who won't side with me to hunt him down. When he's out of the way, we'll be stronger'n ever."

Ace shrugged. "It may work," he said dubiously. "But first I got to see the man who can corral Montana. He's poison."

Frazer's eyes hardened. "Looks to me like you're losin' your guts, Doolin. It looked that way the other day when Pierce made the whole pack of you take water in Singletree."

The grin that crossed Ace's face was a leering one. "You were in on that, too, Ralph. I didn't see you go for leather."

Frazer shrugged, and the look he gave his foreman was inscrutable. "I hire men to make my gun play for me. In case they go yellow, I'll count on my own irons."

The interruption that came was timely. From outside the sound of a horse pounding into the yard echoed loudly. Instinctively Frazer stiffened, drew his Colt, and laid it on the desk. The door burst open and Henry Crossan stood framed in it, his face dust-covered and streaked with sweat, his Levi's foam-flecked from a fast ride.

"Well, Crossan?" Frazer asked, picking his Colt from the desk top and dropping it into his holster.

"I've got news," Crossan said, breathing heavily.

"Must be damned important to bring you five miles at this

time of night. You came in a hell of a hurry, too. Come on, what is it?"

Crossan jerked his head in Doolin's direction, raising his eyebrows in a mute query.

Frazer waved impatiently: "Go on, go on."

"I saw Montana Pierce tonight," Crossan began. "He. . . ."

"You what?" Frazer shouted, rising out of his chair. "Where was he?"

"He came up to where I was ridin' above the line camp."

"Was it a raid?" Frazer snarled. "How many head did they get away with?"

"None," Crossan replied. "Montana came up to see me."

Slowly Frazer eased back into his chair again.

"He's wantin' me to ride with him." Crossan did not look at Frazer as he spoke, but fumbled in his shirt pocket for tobacco, and a match. He did not see the glance Frazer flashed at Ace Doolin, nor the look that passed between them.

"You and Montana were pretty good friends, as I remember it," Frazer said significantly.

Crossan nodded. "He's all right, I reckon. But plumb loco for sittin' in a game that's too stiff for him."

"What did you come here to tell me?" Frazer's impatience could wait no longer.

Henry Crossan did not answer until had lighted his cigarette. When he did speak, his words were flat, pointed. "I've come to claim that reward."

Frazer could not hide his surprise. His eyes narrowed and an ugly grimace contorted his face. "I'll pay that reward when I see Montana Pierce in jail."

"He's yours for the takin'."

"You know where to find him?"

Crossan nodded.

"Where is he?" Frazer asked.

A grin broke over Ace's thin face and he nodded his understanding.

Frazer took on the confidence of a man who has finally topped his last obstacle. All the greed for power and success mounted up within him as he strode about, pompously directing his men. They threw Montana over the saddle of one of the riders and headed back for the Bar Z.

"Ace," Frazer said, pulling in alongside his foreman. "There's not a damned thing to stop us now. What did I tell you?"

Ace shook his head. "You got me, boss. He sure played into our hands."

Frazer laughed strangely then, and in that laugh there was a sinister cruelty that made even Ace shudder.

VI

The moon edged up over the far horizon as the Bar Z riders neared Singletree with their prisoner. In the clear light the adobes of the town were thrown into gaunt relief, the rounded bulk of their low walls with protruding vigas making them look strangely like a colony of fat, overturned beetles. Faint shadows hung in the fog of dust that marked the passage of the riders as they turned into the street and moved on toward the jail.

Montana rode between Ace and Frazer, sitting the saddle with his wrists bound to the horn. As if by mutual consent they had made the ride in silence. Montana had looked behind him only once, and that for the purpose of counting the eight Bar Z gunnies who completed his guard. It was evident that Frazer was taking no chances with his prisoner.

The only lights showing along the deserted street were in the sheriff's office and the saloon. Frazer dismounted before the jail, threw his reins over the hitch rail, and walked over to unlace Montana's wrists. "Don't be damn' fool enough to try a break," he grumbled as Montana swung stiffly to the dusty street and followed him across the walk and up the steps to the sheriff's office. They found the door open, the office empty, with the lamp on the desk casting a circle of yellow light over the meager furnishings.

In addition to the desk there were three chairs, a safe, a bench along the back, and several Reward notices tacked onto the bare walls of the rooms. An alarm clock ticked off the seconds with a tinny, monotonous sound, its hands indicating the hour to be 2:20.

Frazer stepped to the steel door at the rear of the office, tried to turn the handle, but found the door locked. As soon as Ace came in, he said: "Send someone up to Canby's house and tell him to come down here with the keys."

While Ace relayed the message to one of the riders outside, Frazer stepped to the desk, pulled open the drawers, and went through them. Finally he straightened up and came over to Montana and snapped a pair of handcuffs over his wrists.

"You're playing me plenty safe, Frazer," Montana said, grinning broadly.

"I'm playin' to see you swing with your neck in a noose tomorrow," came Frazer's ready answer.

"You've played 'em close all along, haven't you?"

Frazer took a seat in Canby's chair behind the desk before replying. "If you knew me better, you'd know I never play 'em any other way." Frazer leaned back, hands laced over his stomach, casually surveying Montana. There was about him an air of supreme confidence as he reached into his vest pocket for a cigar and bit off the end of it. His eyes did not leave Montana as he lit a match and drew the smoke of his cigar down into his lungs with evident relish. A low chuckle issued from between his parted lips and he said softly: "You damned fool!"

Ace came across the room and sat on the edge of the desk, one foot swinging idly as his cursory glance ran over Montana.

"Supposing I'd called Canby out to see that wet beef we found up at Gabe Halpin's place the other night, Frazer," Montana said. "You'd have had some tall explaining to do!"

Frazer shrugged carelessly. "What do you suppose I pay Canby for?"

"So you do pay him?" came Montana's question, his brows contracted in a look of seriousness. "Careful what you say, Frazer. I might spill a few things at my trial tomorrow . . . if I'm to have a trial."

"You'll get a trial, right enough," Frazer said softly, his gray eyes glinting coldly with amusement. "Only there won't be anyone who'll believe a word you say. Tomorrow's my day, Pierce, and I'm makin' the best of it."

Montana was silent for a moment. As he lifted his shackled hands to his shirt pocket for his tobacco, he flashed a glance at Ace, saw the frown on his lean face as he regarded Frazer. It was what Montana wanted. He spoke again. "When I'm out of the way, you can run hog wild on this range, eh?"

"Why not?" Frazer replied arrogantly, a low chuckle shaking his frame. "Two years from now the Bar Z brand will be runnin' across three counties along the foot of the Antelopes. There's nothin' to stop me."

"Careful, boss," drawled Ace. "You'll be sayin' somethin' out of turn."

"Careful, hell," Frazer snapped, leaning forward in his chair. "What does it matter what he hears? Who's goin' to believe anything an outlaw says? You've built your own hang noose, Pierce. When you dynamited Halfway Wells, you made an enemy of every rancher on the range. Your word won't count any more. Even your friend Crossan went against you . . . turned you over for a reward."

"Crossan's a dirty sidewinder!" Montana exploded, then relapsed into silence for a moment, seeming to be trying to get control of his temper. "But at least you've lost out with your fake homesteaders. You lose four thousand acres."

Frazer raised his hands in a matter-of-fact gesture. "It may slow me a year or so. But that water'll come back. I'll put more men out there next year and buy it eventually."

"Ralph, dammit, you're sayin' things," Ace's warning came again.

"Hobble your tongue, Doolin," Frazer snarled, banging his fist on the desk top. "It's my own damned business what I say here."

Ace muttered under his breath, and sauntered over to the door and stood looking out into the night. It was plain that he had no liking for the turn the conversation had taken.

"That was a hell of a trick you used in framing Clem Walker," Montana said bluntly. "A hell of a trick."

"You broke with me over that, didn't you?" Frazer asked. "Too damned chicken-hearted to back me in that play. I could have used you, too," he mused.

Although the air was chill, beads of perspiration stood out on Montana's high forehead. He shifted a little in his chair with nervousness. "That was too raw," he said, emphasizing his words with a look of loathing. "It wouldn't have worked with anyone but Clem . . . a stranger."

"I counted on that," Frazer said, seeming to find a satisfaction in divulging his misdeeds. "No one here knows or cares much about Walker."

"So you made a rustler out of him."

"I need that Circle W water. It was easy plantin' that herd. Ask Ace. He helped drive it."

Ace shrugged his disgust without turning.

At that moment a key grated in the lock of the door behind Frazer. He was turning in his chair to search out the noise when the door swung open and disclosed Peewee's huge bulk framed in the opening. For an instant Frazer hesitated before his hand dropped to his Colt. In that split second interval Montana lunged, swept the lamp off the desk to the floor.

Behind Montana two deafening shots blended together, and in the light of those gun flashes he saw Ace's .45 sweeping upward. Montana threw his entire weight into the vicious downsweep of his manacled hands and heard the snap of Ace's wrist as the connecting chain hit it. Ace shrieked horribly and Montana caught the six-gun as it flew outward from the impact.

He whirled, sent a snap shot in Frazer's direction, turned back toward Ace just as the Bar Z ramrod's left hand stabbed upward from his left thigh. Ace fired, the gun flash blinding Montana, and sending a searing burn along his scalp as the slug grazed him. Then Montana thumbed the hammer of his own Colt viciously, felt the solid buck of it in his hand. Ace's lean frame crumpled and fell forward out of the moonlit doorway.

Outside, someone yelled, and Montana heard men running across the boardwalk and up the steps. He braced himself, standing in the center of the room, and raised his shackled hands to throw two deadly shots at the figure of a Bar Z gunny who suddenly sprang into the doorway.

A crash of glass blended with the shooting outside as someone moved alongside Montana and kicked out a window. His hopes rose, as he sensed the presence of the others in the room. The next instant the place was a roaring inferno of beating gun blasts. Rand Avery's lean figure was outlined a moment at the window as he gunned down into the crowd of Bar Z riders at the foot of the steps.

The gunnies whipped a hail of lead in through the doors and windows. Montana stepped near a window, peered around the frame, and caught a fleeting glimpse of a man running behind the hitch rail. Montana's Colt sent a purple flame stab into the night and the runner sprawled on his face.

Montana lingered there a split second too long. A slug tore along his right shoulder as he raised his hands again. A burning stab of pain low in his chest took his breath for a moment. He thumbed his Colt once more, but the hollow click of the hammer told him it was empty. In a sudden frenzy he moved away from the window, slowly, for it seemed his muscles had lost their co-ordination.

The stench of powder smoke was strong in the air and bit into his eyes, blurring his vision. All at once a weakness caught him, dragged him down, and he pitched his length across the floor. He tried to cry out, but a blackness blotted his vision. . . .

Peewee Steele's face took form as the fog of unconsciousness cleared from Montana's brain. Montana saw that Peewee was grinning, that his lips were moving. It was an effort to look about, but he did so, seeing that he was lying in bed in a small, neatly kept room. Peewee's words came to him then.

". . . You've been a hell of a long time comin' around, bad man. We figured for a while you might be ridin' herd on the clouds."

It came to Montana that Peewee was telling him that he was sick, that he had narrowly escaped death. "How long have I been here?" he asked feebly.

"Just since mornin'," Peewee told him.

A flood of memory left Montana with a mounting curiosity. "Did we get Frazer?"

Peewee's broad grin disappeared. "We got him," he said haltingly. "He was shot up bad, so we put him on one of the cots in a cell. Sawbones Yates wouldn't let us move him. That was this mornin'. Well, about an hour ago a mob busted in and took him away." He paused significantly, his face drawn and gone a little pale.

Montana could guess the rest. With a sudden recollection he

blurted out: "Where was Canby? Why didn't he have a guard over the jail?"

"The sheriff blew the top off his head this mornin'," Peewee explained. "Grabbed Juan's cutter and did it before we could stop him. I reckon he saw what was comin'."

After a moment Montana asked: "Was Jim Early in on it?"

"Yeah. Henry Crossan rode to get him after he'd first taken Frazer over to find you. Told him he'd have to come to be a witness to a confession. Jim didn't want to miss out on his sleep so he told Henry to get someone else. Henry pulled his iron and brought Jim in anyways. He heard the whole thing from behind the cell-block door. When Frazer told about framin' Clem Walker, I thought he was goin' to claw his way right through door."

"Henry did a good job, Peewee."

"He's shakin' like a quakin' aspen right now. Said he'd cut his throat if you cashed in your chips. He feels sort of responsible for startin' the whole thing. He was like a loco steer, waitin' there in the jail before Frazer showed up with you. Said he didn't see why Frazer wouldn't beef you when he found you all trussed up an' waitin' for him."

"Frazer had to play it big, Peewee," Montana said. "Bringing me to trial would have made him the big augur around here for good, and he knew it." He paused a moment, then asked: "How about the rest? Any charges against any of us?"

"Not a one. Gabe Halpin gets his spread back. Clem Walker's out of jail. Hell, there's talk of runnin' you for sheriff. There's others. . . ." Pewee's words trailed off as he stepped backward to look out of the door into the next room. He grinned broadly as he turned to Montana and said in a low voice: "Here comes someone who wants to see you bad."

Almost before he had finished, Betty Walker came into the room. She stood beside the door for a moment as Peewee awkwardly edged his bulk out through it. For the space of two full seconds she stood there, her loveliness filling Montana with a longing he could not keep from showing in his eyes. Then, abruptly, she came to him, knelt beside the bed, and buried her face at his shoulder, sobbing softly. Presently he took her face between his hands and kissed her.

"I'll never turn you away again, Montana," she said at last, and the smile that sparkled in her eyes told him more than a thousand words.

★ ★ ★ ★ ★

Rust Off a Tin Star

★ ★ ★ ★ ★

"Rust Off a Tin Star" was submitted by the author's agent to *Complete Western Book Magazine* on December 3, 1937. The story was accepted for publication on March 12, 1938. The author was paid $67.50. Upon publication in the May, 1938 issue the title was changed to "An Ex-Marshal Ramrods the *Malpaís*". For its first book appearance the author's original title has been restored.

I

The first time Yace Metten—or anyone in Salt Springs, for that matter—ever laid eyes on Ferd Borch was the day Borch walked into the Prairie State Bank and bought the Broken Stirrup. Jim Yocum, president of the bank, told Metten about it later: "He was slick, Yace, asking me offhanded what outfits were for sale. One look at him and I decided he'd never seen more than a thousand dollars in one pile, so I named him off three or four of those small layouts down Wind Cañon. He claimed he'd looked the country over and wouldn't pick Wind Cañon unless he had to. I was busy and wanted to get rid of him, so, real smart-like, I asked how a thirty section spread would suit him. Like a damn' fool I laid it on thick, acting serious about wanting to sell the Broken Stirrup. Before I knew what happened, he'd pulled ten thousand in greenbacks out of his pants and put it up to cover, either a two year lease or a twenty percent down payment on the layout. I'll be lucky if John Hackett doesn't skin me alive."

Yace Metten was thinking the same. John Hackett would probably take pleasure in nailing friend Yocum's hide to the doors of the bank that had sold the Broken Stirrup out from under him, seeing that he'd spent the last three years wanting the Broken Stirrup and was only waiting for this spring's calf count to be sure he had the $50,000 to spend.

As town marshal, it was Yace Metten's business to know what went on, so when John Hackett drove into town with his daughter the day after the sale, looking mad as a grizzly with a sore paw, Yace kept his eyes open. Things worked out differently than any of them had expected.

Ferd Borch was at the bank, clearing up a few last details of his purchase, when Hackett arrived. No one ever knew what went on in Yocum's office, but an hour later when Yace saw the three of them—Matthews, Borch, and Yocum—go up the street to have a drink at the Silver Dollar, he was surprised to see that all three were smiling and cordial. That was Ferd Borch's way, the marshal learned later; Borch was big and hearty and easy to get on with, and John Hackett had evidently made up his mind that his fifty-six section Split H was big enough for any one man and that he was lucky to draw such a good neighbor.

Before the day was out, Ferd Borch had met Marjorie Hackett. The next Saturday night, Yace dropped in at the dance at the schoolhouse and found Borch there with Marjorie; they made a fine-looking pair. Inquiring around, the marshal discovered that Jerry Brand, who should have been there with the girl, couldn't attend—he'd driven a bunch of fat feeders thirty miles across to the spur of the D&RG and didn't get back. It hurt the marshal a little to see what a good time Marge had with Borch, and without Jerry.

Two weeks later Yace met Jerry Brand in town and had the chance to talk to him. In these past two weeks he had seen Marge Hackett with Borch a half dozen times and didn't like it. Today, taking Jerry Brand down to his office, Yace was a little concerned over the set, worried frown on young Brand's face.

When they had taken chairs in the office, Yace said casually: "It looks like a good year for beef, Jerry. Good snow last winter, not too cold, and now a nice chance of an early spring. All of which proves that the gent who had the guts to stick it out these three bad years is going to cash in after all. You're one of 'em."

Jerry Brand shook his head, his frown not easing. "I've

thought maybe I'd clear out of here in another year, Yace. It looks better farther south."

Metten, always blunt, came to the point: "And leave Marge?"

Jerry shrugged. "That was too good to last."

"So this stranger, Borch, is . . . ?"

"Lay off, Yace," Jerry cut in irritably. He got up out of his chair and sauntered to the door. "I know how you feel about it. Thanks for tryin' to help. But right now no man alive can change Marge's ideas, includin' me." He went out the door, slamming it behind him.

Yace spent a good many minutes that day wondering about those two. He liked Jerry Brand, admired the way he had made the most of a shoe-string start with his JB outfit, and he more than liked Marge Hackett. Better than thirty years ago he had thought he would one day marry Marge's mother, but John Hackett had come to the country a stranger, like Ferd Borch, and she had married John. Years later Yace had buried his loser's grudge and learned to like John Hackett. Now that the mother was dead, he found that the daughter filled in the gap in his affection.

He was wondering if he could ever like Borch. That afternoon, at the Silver Dollar, he had the chance to study the man. The new Broken Stirrup owner was playing poker at a back table with four of his crew, all strangers to this country who had come in within the last few days. Yace watched the game for an hour, studying particularly Borch's play at stud. At the end of that hour Yace was ready to admit that Borch knew his poker; he played with a studied recklessness that consistently piled up his winnings.

As Yace was about to leave, another of Borch's stranger crew, a gray-haired oldster, joined the game. He was small-framed, wiry, gray-eyed, and something hauntingly familiar about the man's thin face and his slouching walk sent Yace back to his office to rummage nervously through a thick sheaf of Reward dodgers, some of them bearing dates of twenty-seven years back. At the end of half an hour he hadn't found what he wanted.

He tilted the back of his chair against the desk and faced the back wall of the room, eyes half closed, thinking. Yace Metten prided himself on an unfailing memory, yet just now it was going back on him. Where had he seen this gray-eyed man of his own generation, and why did he unconsciously associate the gaunt face and that slouching walk with a Reward poster?

Once during his evening meal at the lunch counter down the street he thought he had it, but whatever flash of memory had prompted his thought soon deserted him. He went back to his office instead of going to his hotel room, and sat in the dark, trying to think it out. By 10:00 P.M. he was asleep in his chair.

Three hours later the thinly muted blast of a gun from across the way jerked him into wakefulness. He climbed stiffly out of his chair, at the same time looking out the window to see the lights on in the saloon across the street. Ten seconds later he was shouldering his way through the saloon's swing doors, a wariness making him keep his right hand close to his low-swung six-gun. A casual glance in at the hardware store window on the way over had told him the time—1:05 A.M.

It was past closing time for the Silver Dollar, yet three men were drinking at the bar and four more sat at the back table, Ferd Borch and the gray-eyed oldster two of the quartet. Tim Chester, owner of the saloon, was standing alongside their table, his pear-shaped usually pinkish face drained of color.

Yace walked on back to the table, catching details that had at first passed his notice. Ferd Borch's face was flushed beneath its tan. Sitting on his left, the gray-haired man with the gaunt face was grinning wickedly, tilted back in his chair, looking up at

Tim Chester.

"What's the trouble?" the marshal asked.

Tim Chester breathed a sigh of relief and half turned and said: "I tried to close up, Yace. They won't let me. Hank, the old gent across there, yanked his cutter and shot the heel off my boot when I started out to the hotel to get you."

Yace looked across at the oldster, at that arrogant smile. Once more he was trying to place the man. "Ten years ago the town council drew up an ordinance requiring saloons to close at one o'clock. It's past that now. You gents'll have to clear out." The marshal spoke mildly, seeing that these four had obviously been drinking.

Ferd Borch's tanned face took on a genial grin. "Anything you say, Metten. We were blowin' off some steam, I reckon. We'll leave." He started to rise from his chair.

At that moment, Hank, the oldster Yace Metten had been trying to remember, reached out and pulled Borch back into his chair, growling: "Who the hell says we leave?" He pushed himself onto his feet and kicked his chair out of the way and stood there, spraddlelegged, his right hand within two inches of his gun. For the first time Yace Metten noticed the way the man wore that gun—low-slung and tied down.

All at once Yace had a flashingly clear picture of a day twenty-seven years ago when a wild-eyed four-horse team had run madly down the center of Salt Spring's single street pulling an empty stage and with the dying driver slumped down behind the footboard. Yace remembered a four day ride on an eight-man posse in vain search for a gray-eyed stranger who had a slouchy walk and had suddenly disappeared from town—the man the driver carefully described before he died. Months later, a Montana Reward dodger with the man's picture on it had given Yace the name of Bill Henry, alias Slick Henry, and the warning that Henry was a killer and a fast shot.

During the two-second interval in which Yace recognized the man they called Hank, seven pairs of eyes centered on him, the three men at the bar moving out of line in back of him.

When Yace spoke, his words were toneless, a soft drawl: "I say you leave, friend Hank."

Hank's thin lips curled down in a sneer, and, as his eyes clouded over in a merciless coldness, Yace Metten felt fear for the first time in his life. The Reward dodger had said that Bill Henry was a killer and a fast shot.

"I don't want trouble. Just walk out of here and go home and sleep it off. This place is closed."

"You think you can close it?"

Hank threw the challenge bluntly, and waited. Ferd Borch made no attempt to interfere; instead, he sat there with that smile Yace was beginning to hate, waiting like the rest.

Everything was wrong here. Yace had never before faced a man who had made a thing like this stick. A hot rage boiled up in him, wiping out his fear, all at once steeling him to the fighting recklessness that had brought him through thirty years of cleaning up a hard town and keeping it clean. He had met a dozen glory hunters, a few more who were dangerously fast on the draw, and he was still alive and they were gone. Thinking this, he flashed his hand at his gun.

Timed with his motion, Hank's hand moved. It streaked out his short-barreled Colt and swung it into line in one smoothly timed motion. Ferd Botch lunged and knocked Hank's gun down a full half second before Yace leveled his weapon. Borch twisted the .45 from Hank's hand.

He had lost on the draw, lost badly. The realization brought a fine, beady perspiration to Yace Metten's high forehead. "Thanks, Borch," he drawled. "Now corral your bunch and herd 'em out of here before I let this thing go off."

Hank, rubbing his wrist sprained from Ferd Borch's quick

blow, breathed: "Give me back that cutter, Ferd. This tin star is a joker, and I'll prove it."

Ferd turned to the oldster. "Open your mouth again and I'll break your teeth in with your own iron, Hank." He rammed Hank's weapon through the waistband of his Levi's and looked across at Yace and said: "Forget this, Metten. Hank has a quart of whiskey in his guts."

"Get him out of here." Yace felt a little sheepish about having his gun still in his hand and now dropped it into his holster.

He stood there and watched them leave, Ferd Borch taking Hank by the arm and leading him out through the doors. Hank was cursing loudly, and once looked back at Yace with that same cold, killing light in his eyes.

After the swinging batwing doors had rocked to a stop on their hinges, Yace and Tim Chester listened while the six ponies trotted down the street and on out of hearing. When the sound had died in the night's silence, Tim let out a gusty sigh and said: "That was close, Yace. Too close. You gettin' rusty?"

II

Salt Spring's marshal had more on his mind the next morning than he cared to admit even to himself. He asked himself if Tim Chester had been right: was he getting rusty? Several times after his early breakfast he looked at his gnarled hands; the fingers were long, a little knobby at the knuckles, and now that he thought of it they felt a bit stiff at the joints. Alone in his office, he let his hand palm his heavy Colt up in a draw, as fast as he could; his arm-muscles seemed to lack their old co-ordination and the gun didn't rock steady the way it had years ago. Or was it his imagination? A little sheepishly, he put the gun back and didn't try it again.

So Hank was really Bill Henry? Yace could name all seven men who had ridden out on that posse in the hunt for Slick

Henry; six of those others were dead now—Yace had been the youngest—and George Watt, the seventh, still ran his hardware store but had a failing memory and couldn't even name his grandchildren. Of course, if he wanted to go to the trouble and really go after the facts on Bill Henry, he could get them. But some instinctive wariness warned him to wait; he didn't like Ferd Borch, and, if Hank was any example of the kind of men Borch hired, the outfit would bear watching.

Hank was thinking of this when Sheriff Don Ross opened the door to his office and stepped in. Ross was usually genial, but now his expression was one of worried perplexity.

Before Yace could even say hello, Ross was blurting out: "Rustlers, Yace. One of Jerry Brand's riders just sloped into town to tell me Jerry's missing a herd of a hundred and fifty head that left through his north fence late last night. You want to ride out with me?"

Yace was already out of his chair, reaching for his Stetson on the peg behind the door. As the two of them went out onto the street, the marshal asked: "How did it happen? Anyone see anything?"

"Not one damned thing . . . until sunup this mornin'. Then Billings, riding fence, came across the break. Brand's gone on ahead, following the sign, and we're to catch up with him."

"You taking anyone along?"

Ross gave Yace a sideward glance, a look faintly accusing. "Since when do we two need help, Yace?"

The marshal didn't answer, but his instinct told him that Tim Chester must have let out the story of the showdown in the Silver Dollar last night. Don Ross, an old friend, was looking for the signs of rustiness Tim Chester had mentioned.

It was a two-hour ride. Yace didn't talk much on the way out and Ross was in too much of a hurry to be his usual, loquacious self. At the JB ranch house they picked up one of Jerry's riders who took them four miles farther north, to the limits of JB fence. There, so plain it couldn't be missed, was the broad, trampled sign left by the herd.

Jerry had followed it at a trot; they followed him at a stiff run, Ross so impatient to get this done with that he wasn't thinking much of his horse. It was eleven miles farther on, deep in the hills, that they overtook Jerry Brand.

He was out of his saddle and sitting on a sizeable outcrop along the wide bed of a shallow cañon, smoking. His greeting was curt, although his eyes warmed a bit at sight of Yace. As they stopped in front of him, he announced: "We're goin' to have the same answer this time as we've had the others, Sheriff."

Ross frowned. "How come?"

"It's three more miles to that stretch of *malpaís.* That's where all these other herds have gone, and that's where we'll lose mine."

There hadn't been much time to think this out, but now that Jerry mentioned the *malpaís,* Yace was remembering that every sizeable stolen herd that had disappeared from the Salt Springs range the past five years had headed into the hills and across that stretch of jagged rock with its many cañon offshoots. The county line bisected the *malpaís,* and long ago Ross had learned that Sheriff Benson of the adjoining county wasn't particularly interested in hanging any rustlers. Benson had once or twice offered his help, but on one occasion three days spent in exploring only a dozen of those cañon offshoots had discouraged Benson to the point of doubting Don Ross's word that the herd was hidden up there.

Ross voiced his discouragement at the hopeless task that faced them. "Then you can kiss your critters good bye, Brand."

"If I do, the bank gets my outfit. I'll ride on and have a look."

Brand and his rider led the way, Yace and Ross following. Yace was trying to remember how many cattle had been lost across the *malpaís* during the past five years; before that, rustling was unheard of around Salt Springs. There had been Abe Connor's sixty head four years ago, Brady Mayer's whole herd of prize yearlings the year before, and John Hackett had only last year lost close to three hundred heifers he didn't even bother to look for because his Split H could stand the loss and not miss it. These stolen herds and many more had drifted across the *malpaís* and out of sight. And whoever had swung the sticky loop was being clever about it, for the thefts didn't amount to enough to make the law stand up on its hind legs and make a real try at hunting down the hide-out—a range this big could afford to lose a few hundred head each year. But Jerry Brand was hard hit and Yace knew it only too well. It was a pity Jerry wasn't a big enough man to crack the whip at Ross and make him go across into the next county and round up a posse and do the job right.

Jerry Brand's premonition had been correct. The sign showed strongly all the way to that jagged, black, uneven mass of sharp-edged rock that stretched across a four-mile valley and lost itself in countless offshoots that wound up uncountable side cañons. All four of them reined in and had their look across the *malpaís*, and finally Jerry shifted in his saddle a little to face Ross and queried: "Well?"

Ross lifted his shoulders in a shrug. "It's the same as before, Jerry. They're gone. I'm damned sorry."

Jerry Brand was held wordless in pent-up anger. Yace Metten felt a lesser measure of his young friend's helplessness, only that he was looking into the future and wondering what the bank would say to Jerry's missing his interest payments for another year.

There wasn't a thing to be done about it. Jerry announced a little feebly: "I'll stay up here a couple of days and have a look. You and Yace ride back to town. It's a waste of time for you."

Ross didn't say a thing, but Yace had an idea that made him take Jerry aside and tell him: "I'll be back. Tonight, probably. You meet me here at sundown."

On the ride back to Salt Springs, after they'd eaten their noon meal at the JB bunkhouse and Ross and Yace were alone, Yace broke a long silence to say: "Don, there's something I've had on my mind a good while. I'm too old for my job. This town needs a younger man for marshal."

For a full ten seconds Sheriff Ross was silent. Then: "If you're thinking about what happened last night, forget it. It was a fluke."

"No, it wasn't. This jasper, Hank, could have blown my guts out if it hadn't been for Ferd Borch. I'm slowing up, Don."

"At your age, a man's got a right to slow up, ain't he?"

Here it was, a tactful admission that was as damning as a blunt accusation. But Yace didn't mind, and went on: "That's what I've been thinking. This afternoon I'll see Ben Baker and turn in my resignation. The council can hire another man. Maybe that youngster from down by Niles City would do. But here's something else, Don. This afternoon, after I've resigned, I'm coming to you for a job."

"A job?" Ross glanced across at his friend, puzzled.

"I want a deputy sheriff's badge, Don."

"You . . . what!"

"For thirty years I've been tied down by the town limits. There's been plenty of times I've wanted to work out in the county and had to come to you or the half dozen other sheriffs I've known before you. I want to help a friend this time, and with a deputy badge to back me."

"You mean Brand? You're buying into his troubles?"

Yace nodded savagely.

"But all you had to do was ask. You don't have to quit as marshal."

"It doesn't have a thing to do with that. Last night proved a lot that's wanted proving. Hell, Don, it's the first time I've had to go for my cutter in nearly two years. I'm through."

In the presence of such bluntness, Don Ross couldn't find any words to express what he felt. He, like a lot of others, would hate to see Yace Metten go. Yace was part of the town, damn it. But a lot of others would be howling at Yace's heels when the story of last night got around, and maybe Yace was wise in being forehanded about the whole thing.

The rest of that ride was embarrassing for both men, and for different reasons they were glad when it was over. With Yace, it was because he was in a hurry. The first thing he did was to go to Ben Baker's newspaper office and turn in his resignation and his badge. When Ben protested, Yace cut him short. "This is final, Ben. I quit tonight. Your new man can take over the office. All I've got to move is junk. It can wait for a couple days."

At 3:30 he stopped in at the sheriff's office. Ross protested: "I'm damned if I know why I'm letting you do this, Yace." But when Yace held out his hand for the badge lying on Ross's desk, the sheriff gave it to him and mumblingly repeated the oath of office and swore in his new deputy. Ten minutes later, Yace was leaving town, riding north toward the JB.

He met Jerry Brand on the edge of the *malpaís* shortly after dark that evening. They had little to say during their meal, or afterward, and they turned in early. Yace didn't sleep much that night.

Up before dawn the next morning, Yace announced over breakfast: "You've got your work cut out for you, friend. I'd start off here to the right, with that first side cañon. Work all of it. When you're finished, go on to the next. Take 'em as they come and don't miss a one, no matter how small it looks. I've seen a mile-wide valley opening out of a crack in a boulder."

Jerry Brand was puzzled and his look showed it. "You aren't comin' with me?"

Yace shook his grizzled head. "There's another little job I've got on my hands."

After a moment's silence, Jerry asked: "Anything you can tell me?"

"Yesterday I happened to remember that time eight, ten years ago when I arrested young Blaine Benson. You remember . . . the brother of Sheriff Benson across in the next county." Yace pointed across the *malpaís* to the imaginary county line. "Well, at the time we thought this Benson hombre had knifed a Mexican in a row over the Mexican's wife, seeing as how Benson had been riding to Salt Springs nearly every week to see her. The Mexican was dead, and we didn't have anything much to prove the killing, but I arrested him. I was getting ready to look into it when Benson's brother, the sheriff, paid us a call. Not me . . . because he wouldn't have gotten as far with me . . . but he powwowed with a few of our upstanding citizens, and the first thing I knew they came to me with a proposition. I was to release this Benson in exchange for a man we wanted who was hiding in the next county . . . a gent called Texas Mike, who had busted up a saloon and killed a bartender."

"You were to let young Benson go, then, without preferring charges against him?"

"That's right." Yace pulled at his pipe and got it going, and went on. "This law game's a funny one, Jerry. I've always aimed to keep clear of tics, but this is one time I couldn't. It seems that Sheriff Benson had known all along that this Texas Mike was in that hide-out up near Baldy Peak. The hide-out's a regular town . . . stores and saloons and maybe a dozen cabins . . . and every sidewinder this side of the Colorado River has been up there at one time or another, hiding from the law.

It would take a regiment to take the town, and Benson has always had sense enough not to try it.

"I wanted Texas Mike, and I didn't have proof against Benson's brother. And I didn't think the sheriff could deliver Texas Mike. So I offered to make the trade, holding young Benson until his brother delivered the man I wanted. I didn't think he could do it, but he did. He took me up there, clear to the edge of that town. He had me wait there, and after half an hour he came ridin' back with Texas Mike. Mike was dead, slung across Benson's saddle. I had to let the brother go."

"But how could he go in there and take this Texas Mike?"

Yace shrugged his bent shoulders. "I've never known. But since then I've heard something that makes the sheriff out as little better than some of those owlhooters that live up at the hide-out. It's this. Blaine Benson is up there now, running the biggest saloon in the town, and I'm going up after him."

Jerry Brand's mouth gaped open in sheer astonishment. "You're what?"

"I want a talk with Blaine Benson. I'm going up there."

A subtle change rode over Jerry Brand. A moment ago his amazement had been obvious. Now he was obviously disappointed. He didn't have anything to say, and, knowing what was on his mind, Yace made haste to add: "If anyone knows who's been rustling Salt Springs beef, it ought to be Blaine Benson. Jerry, it's the only way there is to get your herd back."

Quick comprehension showed in Jerry's eyes, and along with it blazed a light that was good to see—a light that showed Yace there was still fight in his friend. Jerry said flatly: "When do we start?"

"I start as soon as I can saddle. But I'm going alone."

"You aren't." Jerry shook his head. "This is a two-man job."

"I thought you'd say that. No, it's a job for one man. I can ride in there and not be bothered. I know my way. You stay here and tend to your knitting. I may be wrong about this. Maybe you'll find where the herd is hidden, and maybe I'm headed up a blind alley. If we split, we'll be drawing two cards to a no-good hand. If we go together, we'll be drawing only one."

It was agreed. They were to meet here three nights from now. In half an hour Yace Metten was out of sight, skirting the *malpaís* for a little-known trail that would take him west, farther into the hills. If he rode hard, he'd be within sight of that hill town hide-out before dark, he had said.

Jerry Brand started half-heartedly on his job of exploring the maze of cañons that ringed the *malpaís* bed. Halfway up the first cañon he turned and rode back to its mouth.

Ross and his posse worked this side last year and didn't find a thing, he mused, remembering the time John Hackett's herd had disappeared. So, instead of beginning his work in his own country, he spent three hours skirting the *malpaís* and working the valley from the far end.

Midafternoon saw him facing the high end wall of a small box cañon, his third since starting. The floor of this cañon was bare rock, and even for the chill of the late winter the reflected sun glare had made the going hot.

He was about to turn and head back down the cañon when his glance traveled up the sheer rock face of the end wall. High above the upthrust point of a massive finger rock whose broad base was directly before him, he saw a zigzag split in the wall, with the blue sky showing through it. It was then he remembered Yace Metten's words: *I've seen a mile-wide valley opening out of a crack in a boulder.*

He knew what he was going to find even before he rode around the base of the tall finger outcropping. Behind it was a ten-foot wide passage between the sheer, vertical walls that had parted centuries ago. And beyond, framed by the jagged sides of the climbing wall, he could get a narrow glimpse of a green, fertile valley.

A flood of wariness prompted him to wheel his chestnut about and start from behind the outcropping. But before his pony had taken a full stride, a voice from high above sounded brittlely across the utter silence: "Hold it, stranger! Lift your paws away from that iron!"

His instinctive gesture toward his holstered six-gun stopped halfway toward its completion. There was menace in that ringing voice, and he was no fool. He looked up, and high above saw the glint of sunlight reflected from a rifle barrel. Above it he made out the vague shape of a man's down-tilted head.

"Ride right on through, stranger," came the voice.

Jerry Brand rode right on through.

III

Yace Metten had stretched his story to Jerry, but only to carry his point. Eight years ago, Sheriff Benson hadn't taken him clear up to the hill town that was the outlaw hide-out. He'd left him a mile or so below, and Yace remembered that he'd tried to follow and hadn't gotten far before a man armed with a rifle stopped him along a narrow ledge trail.

It was late afternoon and Yace had ridden hard all day, and now he climbed up onto that same ledge trail of eight years ago. Around a shoulder of this high, craggy mountain lay the town. This was the only way in, unless a man chose to climb the summit of the peak and go down the far side. There was an old rumor of a man having done that—a lawman—and not knowing what to do after his three-day climb put him within sight of the town. He had wanted to go back, and couldn't; he had gone on, down into the town, and two days later they'd ridden him out the ledge trail tarred and feathered, astraddle a barked cedar limb, with slivers ramming him at every step his lead horses took. He had gone completely mad when they found him four days later. He never told what he knew and no sheriff since then had wanted to find out.

Swinging onto the trail, Yace spurred his tired gray into a stiff trot, having planned what he would do if they tried to stop him. He pulled his Stetson low over his eyes, squared his shoulders to the straightness of a younger man, and rode on, hoping for the best.

He had gone a hundred yards when he heard a sound of sifting gravel up ahead and saw a rider slope down off the high bank in front to block the trail. Yace came on, not slowing the pace of the gray.

Twenty feet short of the guard, he pulled in abruptly, swore with feeling, and growled: "Benson said he'd tell you. I'm late now. Let me pass!"

He made as if to ride around the guard, but the man wheeled his pony into the way and said stridently: "Hold on!" His rifle was raised halfway to his shoulder. "Who the hell is Benson?"

"Blaine, damn it! It's about that herd of Brand's from over in the next county. Can you show me where Benson lives?"

The guard frowned, obviously considering what he should do. This stranger's story sounded right enough. "What herd?" He lowered the rifle and the suspicion was dying in his glance.

Yace cursed again. "All I want is to see Blaine. Either take me in and show me where he lives, or let me pass so someone else can do it. He said for me to meet him at his cabin."

"Sure," the rider agreed, now satisfied. "Only don't be so proddy, granddad." He grudgingly wheeled his pony about and led the way in along the trail. Another hundred yards and the ledge made a right-angle bend—and now the broad gulch that held the town in the lap of its V-shaped bottom lay plainly before Yace Metten. The rider stopped, pointed to the far, tree-margined side of the gulch a quarter of a mile above. "See the shack with the gray roof, the one with the two brick chimneys?

That's Benson's. He's likely up there eatin' his supper now."

Yace didn't wait, but mumbled a surly thanks and rode on, putting his gray to a trot so as to keep up the appearance of being in a hurry. After he had gone a good ways he looked back; the guard was already out of sight around the bend in the trail.

Salt Springs' ex-marshal didn't know what to do from here on. The gulch had broadened out and now trees were growing closely alongside the trail. He took one more look at the cluster of shacks up ahead, where a blue fog of smoke hung above the treetops, and then cut off the trail and headed into the shelter of the cedars. Whatever he was to do would have to wait until dark. It wouldn't be a long wait, for the gulch already lay in shadow, the sun playing its last orange light across the snow-capped peaks three thousand feet above.

In half an hour, when the darkness was complete, Yace was ready to move on. He gave up the idea of skirting the town, not knowing what he would find higher up the walls of the gulch. He felt fairly safe as he rode up the trail in the darkness and walked his gray between the first shacks that edged the town's crude street. His hat was pulled low and he was trying to sit straight and he hoped no one would know him.

Riding past the lights of the saloon was the worst moment of all. He was thankful that this was the supper hour, that only one lounger sat on the wide porch in front of the saloon. This man appeared to be dozing, but as Yace rode past he was hailed—"Howdy, stranger."—and he growled back his own curt greeting and rode on. The lounger stayed where he was, whistling softly now, not even looking at Yace.

He came out of the saddle in front of the shack with the two chimneys. It sat perched a dozen feet above the far end of the street, and in the darkness Yace had a hard time climbing the crude plank steps that led to its door. But the light from a single window guided him and he didn't hesitate; once he had

stepped up onto the narrow stoop before the door, he reach
for the knob and twisted it and pushed it open, stepping in a
palming his weapon from his holster in one lithe motion.

Two people turned at his entrance. The first, a man sitting
a table in one corner with a forkful of beans halfway to his op
mouth, looked up and let the beans drop back into his pla
This was Blaine Benson, older than Yace remembered him, b
with the same shifty blue eyes and the unruly crop of yell
hair that hung down alongside his right eye. The other was
woman, pretty in a hard way, standing before a stove along t
back wall. She was holding a large spoon in her hand and w
stirring something in a kettle, and, as she turned and saw t
gun in Yace's hand, she dropped the spoon and caught h
breath and said: "Blaine, get him!" Then, seeing that h
husband was as helpless as she, she glared across at Yace a
snapped out: "What do you want? Put that gun down."

Yace was looking at the man. "I came up for a talk, Bens
Remember me?"

"You're Metten, from Salt Springs." Benson's voice was sha

Yace advanced three steps that put him alongside Bens
and he reached down and flicked a holstered gun from t
man's thigh, ramming it in his own belt. Then he looked acr
at the woman and said: "Take this chair, please. I want it so t
I can see you both at once."

She breathed a coarse oath and told him: "I stay wher
am."

"Rose, get over here and sit," Benson snarled, not taking
eyes off Yace's gun.

The woman surlily took the other chair at the table. Y
dropped his gun back into its holster and went over to sit on
only other seat in the room, a dirty-blanketed bed. He took
his pipe and filled it.

"Benson, I've come up to take you back with me. T

Mexican woman talked."

"The hell she did," Benson growled. "She don't even live there these days."

Yace hadn't thought of that, so he said easily: "She's down in Santa Cruz. I've been down to see her."

"See here," Benson exploded, "she never did tell the truth. She wants to make trouble for me."

A subtle change rode over the woman's face. She had been angry and sullen a moment ago. Now a trace of suspicion edged into her eyes.

"Benson, I came up here to take you back . . . unless you make a trade with me. What I want to know is where I can find Jerry Brand's herd that was stolen last night. I'll either take his critters back or you. Make your choice."

"Blaine, I want to know what he means . . . this other woman," the wife cut in, staring hard at her husband.

"Tell her, Benson," Yace taunted.

"That was years ago, Rose. Before I knew you. I haven't seen her for eight, ten years."

"That makes a good story, Benson."

The woman, egged on by the thing Yace had implied, sat there with an obvious loathing in her eyes as she regarded her husband.

The strain was too much. Benson lunged to his feet, his fists clenched, his hard stare focused on Yace. "You'll damn' well tell her you lie, tin star. Tell her the truth."

Yace didn't speak, but instead watched the woman. A storm of passion was making her ugly now. It was better luck than Yace had hoped for, pitting these two against each other.

Benson stared about him helplessly, finally sat down with all the fight gone out of him. "All right, Metten. I talk. Only when I'm done, you'll tell her the truth about Panchita." He swallowed thickly and went on: "Brand's cattle are on Borch's range,

back in the hills four miles behind his layout."

"Borch's?" Yace couldn't believe his hearing. "What's Ferd Borch got to do with this?" All at once he was remembering Hank, the Bill Henry of twenty-seven years ago. The posse had followed Henry into the next county that time, had read his sign well up into the hills before they lost it. Unless he was guessing wrong, Bill Henry had come up here. Had he stayed here all these years? Before the thought congealed, he was asking: "How long has Ferd Borch been swinging a sticky loop?"

"A long time," the woman answered him, still eyeing her husband with that cold, uncompromising stare.

"He's been working with Bill Henry?" Yace asked.

"Who's Bill Henry?" This from Benson.

"He knows Bill Henry as well as I do," the woman said scornfully. "Sure Ferd's been working with him, maybe for five years, maybe longer. Anything else you want to know, lawman?"

"Where did Ferd Borch get the money to buy the Broken Stirrup?"

Before Yace had an answer to his questions, he heard the knob of the door rattle softly. He lunged up off the bed and was stabbing his hand at his holstered Colt when Ferd Borch kicked the door open and stood in its opening with two guns at his hips, lined at Yace.

"Where did I get the money to buy the outfit?" Ferd drawled tauntingly. "Why don't you ask me, Metten?"

"All right, where?" Yace was standing rigid, watching for a chance he already knew wouldn't come.

Borch didn't answer. His face broke into that false grin Yace was learning to dislike so much. He jerked his head and muttered—"Bring him in, Hank."—and he stepped aside and two more figures were silhouetted by the lamplight as they stepped in after Ferd.

The first was Jerry Brand, hatless, a bloody smear along one side of his face, his hands tied in front of him with a rawhide thong, and a gag in his mouth; the second, the one who came in after him shoving him roughly into the room, was the oldster, Hank.

Hank looked across at Yace and said: "This is fine. Now I can finish takin' you apart, tin star."

"Easy on the talk, Hank," Ferd Borch ordered. "Get around in back and watch things."

Yace was surprised at seeing how meekly Hank obeyed. Evidently the oldster wasn't so ready to cross Borch when he was sober. After Hank had gone out, Borch pushed Jerry down onto the bed behind Yace, and then faced the marshal. "You were asking where I got my money?"

Yace stood there, looking up at the man—Borch was half a head taller—and wondering why he hadn't suspected something wrong about him a week or so ago, when he began bringing in his hardcase crew. The purpose of the Broken Stirrup was plain now. Borch would use it as his headquarters for his rustlers; he'd never work it. He wondered, too, why Marge Hackett hadn't seen through Borch.

"So you won't talk," Borch went on mockingly. "Suppose I tell you where I got my money. Suppose I tell you anything you want to know. It won't make much difference about the way things. . . ."

"Ferd," the woman cut in, "I want to know who the woman is Blaine's been seeing!"

Borch looked across at her. "What woman?"

A subtle change came over Rose. The look she fastened on Borch had that same measure of scorn in it that she had turned on her husband a minute ago. "So you're helping him. You take him away from here, pretending he's away on business, and all that time he's been seeing her."

"Rose, you're loco."

Benson stepped in between them and pushed Rose roughly aside and stood before Yace. "This old buzzard's faked a story that got her riled," he said softly. He reached down and yanked his gun from Yace's belt, and then lifted Yace's own weapon out of the holster. Then, taking both guns in his left hand, he struck Yace a blow fully in the face with his right—a driving smash that threw Yace back onto the bed beside Jerry Brand.

Yace staggered to his feet and made a vain attempt to reach out for Benson but Borch stepped in and pushed him back onto the bed. "Hold on, you two. Let me get this straight. What sort of a story have you faked for Benson's wife, Metten?"

Slowly Yace put a check on his temper. He answered evenly: "You wouldn't know Panchita, Ferd. You're too new in this country."

"Panchita!" Rose blazed, facing her husband. "Blaine, you can't do this to me!"

"Get over there and sit down at the table, both of you." Borch spoke sharply. "You can settle your quarrel after we're through with this other." He stood looking down at Yace. "Now, Metten, what I want to know is this. Are you alone?"

Before Yace could frame his answer, Rose said seriously: "He's not, Ferd. There were others out there when he came in."

"She's lyin'," Benson put in.

Ferd turned to Benson. "This is a fine time for you two to double-cross me."

"God Almighty, Ferd, I wouldn't double-cross you. Rose, here, she's gone. . . ."

Rose's piercing scream drowned out his words. She lunged to her feet, her two eyes wide, one hand pointing rigidly toward the door behind Borch.

As Ferd turned, she swept the lamp off the table, and it crashed in a brittle, smashing sound of broken glass. The last thing Yace Metten saw before the absolute darkness blanketed out his sight was Rose's hand stabbing at the gun rammed through her husband's belt.

In a flash, Yace had it. The woman, infuriated at what Yace had implied through his mention of Benson's eight-year-old love, was giving him his chance. In her blind jealousy, she was betraying her husband.

On the heel of Ferd Borch's wheeling toward the door, Yace reached out and put all his weight behind a push that sent Jerry Brand falling sideways off the end of the bed. Then Yace was on his feet, crossing the room in two long strides. He collided with a soft body, reached out, and felt that it was Rose.

"Here," she whispered, and he felt the cold steel of a gun barrel thrust into his hand.

The instant he took it, Ferd Borch cursed softly and called—"Hank!"—and the room was lit feebly for a split second by the stab of a gun flame timed with the head-splitting thunder of a .45. Ferd had fired at the bed. Yace reached out and swept the woman behind him with his left hand, and waited. He hadn't seen the powder flash of Borch's gun and he wasn't trusting himself to shoot blindly.

The room went quiet, a hush so pronounced that Yace distinctly heard Benson's breathing off to his left. But he wasn't thinking of Benson; Borch was his man, and one of them would leave the other behind, dead.

A small, scraping sound across by the bed broke the long-drawn stillness. That would be Jerry Brand shifting in his awkward position on the floor. Then, suddenly, a crashing of broken glass sounded as the window on the back wall shattered inward.

"Don't shoot, Hank!" Ferd Borch shouted, so close that Yace felt that he could have reached out and touched the man.

This was the time to act—before Borch moved into him. Yace took one long second to reach back and put his hand on the woman's shoulder and push her down so that she knelt behind him. Then, with his left hand, he swept a long arc out to his side. When it touched Ferd Borch, Yace swung his six-gun around and let his thumb slip off the hammer. A blasting crescendo of sound filled the room; by the gun flash he saw Ferd Borch's backward stagger as the bullet hit him. Then he stepped far back along the wall, barely in time to dodge from between two licking tongues of flame that blasted out at him. Borch and Blaine Benson had both fired at his outline.

In the small silence that followed that terrific concussion, he heard Benson's pulpy, groaning cough and the scraping sound of the man's body as he staggered against the back wall. In another second there was a dull thumping as something hard banged the boards of the floor. Yace guessed that Benson was down. Ferd Borch's bullet had hit his own man.

"Step out and take it, Metten," Ferd Borch drawled softly. His voice was strained to a high pitch, broken by his unsteady breathing. Somewhere in his body, Yace's well-aimed bullet was setting up a torture that was making it hard for him to talk. Instead of that voice sounding from alongside Yace, it now came from across the room, from the direction of the bed.

The woman sobbed softly, realizing what those sounds from over in Benson's corner meant. "Blaine!" she cried brokenly. "Answer me, Blaine!"

Yace felt a movement behind him and heard her crawling along the wall toward where her husband lay. He moved out of line with her, not wanting to draw Borch's fire her way.

Suddenly, from across the room, came the muffled creak of bedsprings. Yace was about to swing his .45 in that direction, when the bed suddenly gave way in a wood-splitting crash as it collapsed heavily to the floor.

"Let him have it, Yace."

It was Jerry Brand who cried out. Somehow he had managed

to get the gag out of his mouth and trip Ferd Borch.

Yace swung his .45 into line, and thumbed a shot toward the head of the bed, well out of line with where he had placed Brand's voice. By the flash of that shot he saw that he had missed, but it clearly outlined Ferd Borch's sprawled figure, and showed Borch swinging his weapon up.

Each one saw the other, each fired in a frantic haste to beat the other's shot. The two explosions blasted out as one. Yace felt a crushing blow high on his thigh, and distinctly felt the grating of a bone as the bullet crashed into it. But his instinct told him that his bullet had smashed into Ferd Borch's chest, and he wasn't often wrong about his gun.

He staggered back against the wall, his right leg going numb and giving way beneath him. It was standing that way, with his back to the wall, that he heard the striking of metal on wood at the back window. He turned to look, and in that instant a blaze of gunfire blinded him. By that gun flash Hank's head was clearly outlined in the opening, that same wicked grin of the previous night stamped clearly on his gaunt face.

Hank had fired that one shot to give him the look of the room. Knowing that, Yace Metten lunged out from the wall as he swung his heavy .45 into line at his hip. He waited for Hank's second shot a split second later, and, when it came, lancing its stab of flame at the spot where he had been, Yace took his time at lining at the shadowed shape of Hank's head. Then he let his thumb slip from the hammer.

One shot, that was enough. He was already stepping out toward Jerry Brand when he heard Hank's body slide down against the wall outside. His right leg supported him nicely now, and, as he stepped out, his foot touched Jerry.

As he knelt over Jerry, taking out his clasp knife so that he could cut the thongs about his friend's wrists, he heard the woman moving about behind him.

Jerry said softly: "The horses are out back. We'd better leave through the window."

Out front and down the trail toward the settlement a man was shouting. The town had heard the gunfire, and now men out there would be getting up the courage to come and investigate. And if they found an ex-marshal, a deputy sheriff, with two of their friends dead from his gun, it didn't take much guessing to see what would happen. There wasn't much time, for a moment later came the sounds of men running up the road, followed by shouts.

His wrists free, Jerry sat up. "I'll get Borch's iron," he said, and crawled down alongside the broken bed. Yace knelt there ten seconds and shucked the empties out of his weapon and reloaded. Then, stepping to the front door, he opened it a slit and fired two quick shots over the heads of a group of shadowy figures running up the road toward the shack. They stopped, turned, and dived for cover. He closed the door, shot the bolt, and crossed the room to the back window.

Jerry was waiting there for him, and had already swung open the broken sash. He boosted Jerry up and through the opening, and was about to follow. Suddenly the woman spoke.

"You tricked me, you forked badge-toter! Blaine didn't have a woman. Now you've killed him. I've killed him!" Her voice was hard, grating, and hushed by the run of a fierce emotion.

Yace heard her moving off there in the corner of the room. For a moment he felt a shame at the way he had tricked her, but she had chosen this life and had to take what it gave her, and Yace had used the only way out. He reached up to the window and pulled himself up, and was halfway through it when a gun crashed behind him.

The bullet whipped the air past his face and splintered the frame at his shoulder, and one sharp needle of wood slashed at his neck. Rose had found her husband's gun and was turning it on the man who had shaped her tragedy.

Yace went on through the window in a sprawling dive. Behind him the woman's gun spoke sharply, once, twice—four times—as she frantically emptied it. Yace fell heavily on one shoulder, but his fall was broken by a giving, soft bulk that was Hank's slumped body lying at the base of the wall.

Jerry Brand pulled him to his feet and helped the lawman along toward the vague outlines of the trees farther up the slope. The thirty seconds it took Jerry to locate the horses seemed an eternity; finally they were in the saddle and riding back through the trees, climbing a little higher along the gulch's sloping side before skirting the town. Back of them and below, from the cabin, came the sound of someone striking the bolted door with the butt of a gun, shouting stridently: "Open up!"

"Ride, Jerry," Yace growled, knowing that the woman would soon give the story to these others.

They were beyond the town, swinging down and into the trail that led out, around the ledge. Both men knew that a guard would try to stop them. But neither knew that this guard would stand dumbly in the trail's center, holding up an arm for them to stop, not realizing who they were.

They both swung up their guns and fired a single shot each. And the guard's rifle dropped from his hands and he doubled at the waist and sloped out of the saddle, his pony shying off the trail and out of the way.

They rode hard that night, stopping once to bandage Yace's leg, which hurt worse than he had let on. Once they thought they heard the far hoof muttering of riders behind, but now they were down into the low foothills and they changed direction, and from then on it was easy going.

At sunup, skirting the four-mile stretch of the *malpaís* bed, Jerry turned to Yace and said, a little sheepishly: "I walked right into it."

"So did I." Yace frowned against the pain in his leg. "You still plan on pulling out of the country after roundup, Jerry?"

Brand grinned. "And leave Marge?" He shook his head, then: "You still figure to give up your badge, Marshal?"

Now it was Yace's turn to shake his head. He was serious. "You know, Jerry, I reckon I was a bit rusty. But after tonight I feel oiled-up again. There isn't another man in this country, young or old, who can hold down that job. I reckon I'll go around to Ben Baker and have him tear up that resignation. You may have to put in a word for me."

★ ★ ★ ★ ★

Nester Payoff

★ ★ ★ ★ ★

In late 1936, Marguerite Harper, Jon Glidden's agent, made a deal with Harry Widmer, managing editor of *Western Trails* magazine, to buy one story for this magazine by each of her three Western fiction authors: Luke Short (Jon's older brother Fred Glidden), Peter Dawson, and T.T. Flynn. "Nester Payoff" was Jon Glidden's title for this story. It was accepted on May 7, 1937 and he was paid $58.50 upon publication in the June, 1937 issue in which the title was changed to "Hell-Born Hatred". The author's original title has been restored for its appearance here.

Dust in endless swirling clouds blanketed the buckboard as Joe Overton reined in the team and looked across toward the foot of the cutbank.

"Why did you kill her, Son?" he asked in a voice muffled by the bandanna bound about his face.

The boy sitting beside him on the seat shifted his spare body a little nervously as his glance followed his father's. A dead cow lay there in the sand, close to a clump of sage, her ribs showing through her dust-caked hide.

"She wasn't as gaunt as the rest," he answered. "We need the meat and she was going to die anyway, with that broken leg."

"I know, I know," the father said. "But killing another man's critter makes you a rustler, Andy. Never forget that. I've seen enough men cash in at the end of a rope to know what it means."

As he spoke, he stepped down onto the wheel hub and eased himself to the ground. Then his tall frame lost its erectness in a stoop-shouldered attempt to ease the obvious pain of each step as he hobbled over to the cow. Joe Overton was a hopeless cripple.

After a single cursory glance at the dead animal, he called back to the boy: "Bring over that axe and the big knife!"

Andy reached into the box under the seat and lifted out a short-handled axe and a thin-bladed butcher knife and took them to his father.

"You shouldn't have come up here in the first place," Joe said as he went to work. "Brad Irick is looking for an excuse to make trouble. This would give it to him."

"We've been skinning out his steers for a week . . . ," the boy began. But then he saw the glint in his father's eye and checked his words.

"Skinning the hide off a dead critter and selling it to keep us from starving means that much less for the coyotes. This is different. We're . . . we're taking a man's beef."

Joe ended lamely, not quite able to explain what he meant, and the boy, seeing the father's hesitation and wanting to defend his own part in this, put in quickly: "Brad Irick steals, doesn't he? That's the way he built up his outfit. You've told me so yourself, Dad. He's the one that took those fifty head of yearlings from Tom Holman day before yesterday."

Joe nodded: "I reckon he does swing a wide loop. But that's no excuse for us. Besides it wasn't Brad Irick this time. Harry Lemon and Big-Lip Hendricks took them critters of Holman's. They got women and babies to feed. We'll make out a while longer."

"Where'd they hide 'em?" the boy asked, immediately interested. Big-Lip Hendricks and Harry Lemon were neighbors who lived a mile or so up the cañon from the Overtons' slab shack.

Joe shrugged his shoulders, answering gruffly: "How would I know? I'd go butcher one for us if I did. You be quiet and let me get at this."

In dutiful silence, the thirteen-year-old boy stood for half a minute watching his father work, passively thinking that things were getting pretty bad when his father would let anyone steal from his friend, Tom Holman. But in times like these it was every man for himself, and the big ranchers like Holman could expect this sort of thing.

He looked off into the smear of dust that hid the range, feeling the oppressive heat and dully aware of the thirst and discomfort that had been with him for days. For seven weeks now, Andy Overton and his father had seen the sky to the north and east banked with ever-climbing dark gray cloud masses.

For seven weeks this insistent sighing breeze had swept the range, at first fanning the moisture from the soil and then gathering up the soil itself to leave the bunch grass roots dotting the rolling sweep of land with small scattered mounds as far as the eye could see.

Of all the people on this range, the boy and his father had the least to lose. A wild bronco and a faithless woman had made a nester's son of Andy. The one had broken his father's body, making him useless as a rider; the other had broken Joe Overton's heart when she deserted him one day, long ago, for another man.

The boy could remember the woman—he never thought of her as his mother—and even now he would occasionally catch his father staring at him with a haunting memory lurking behind his eyes. Joe Overton had once told Andy that he looked like his mother. And the boy had not been proud.

Lately, while the crews of the big outfits spent every waking hour hauling water to their gaunted herds, the Overtons had started skinning out the dead critters and selling the hides to shady Charlie Enders in town; they made enough to buy flour and coffee and sugar. Because he couldn't see more than five rods through the pall of dust, and because the relentless whine of the breeze rose above all the small sounds, Andy didn't see or hear the two riders until they were close in to the cutbank and had already spotted the buckboard.

With sight of them, he breathed a frantic—"Dad."—and the tenor of his voice brought Joe Overton to his feet with the dripping knife still clutched in his hand.

They could only stand there and stare at Brad Irick as he

reined in his chestnut twenty feet away. There was no time to run. The second rider, Hal Corliss, one of Irick's men, hung farther back, seeming to sense what was coming.

After five long seconds of sitting his saddle with an unblinking stare fixed on them, Irick drawled: "Now don't tell me that cow fell down and broke her leg."

"She did!" the boy cried. "I found her here this morning, down. . . ."

"Shut up, Andy," Joe cautioned. Then, looking at Brad Irick, he said: "What the boy says is right. Andy shot her to put her out of misery."

The rancher's broad sun-blackened face twisted into a smile that had no mirth in it. "And you had the guts to bring a rig over to haul the meat home in."

"I can explain all this," Joe put in hastily. "I'll work out what she's worth if you say, but. . . ."

Irick's roar of laughter cut off the words. "Listen to him, Hal," he said, speaking to his rider. "He's goin' to work it out . . . with that crippled leg." He paused for a moment while his countenance went grimly sober. "For two years I've warned you off the Hacksaw, Overton. You and the rest of those nesters. You've got this comin'."

In awed fascination Andy and Joe Overton watched Irick's hand go surely to his thigh to lift a heavy Colt .45 from its holster. Joe reached out and pulled his boy behind him. The color drained from his lean face. As the weapon swung up, he shouted hoarsely: "You can't do this, Irick! You can't . . . !"

The blasting roar of the gun chopped off his words. His tall frame quivered once with the impact of the bullet. And then his hand fell limply from his son's arm. As his weight sagged onto his crippled leg, he fell sideways, half turning to sprawl on his back and stare up at Andy with disbelief in his already glazing eyes.

Irick came down out of his saddle and was almost within reach when Andy tore his horror-stricken gaze from the red splotch of blood spreading across his father's shirt. He darted sideways to elude the rancher's outstretched hands and stooped to snatch the butcher knife from out of his father's limp fingers.

The two of them struck at the same instant. And the heavy gun smashing solidly against Andy's jaw suddenly spun from Irick's grasp as the knife slashed the arm behind it, severing a tendon. The boy went down under that blow, senseless to Irick's ringing oaths as his crippled arm dropped helplessly to his side. In a fury of rage, Irick kicked viciously at the limp form on the ground with blunt, spurred heels.

Hal Corliss ran in and fought Irick back and slapped him across the face twice to bring him to his senses once more.

"Lay off, Brad!" he snapped. "Get something around that arm or there'll be three jobs for the undertaker." He pulled his own knotted bandanna from his face and wound it around Irick's bloody shirt sleeve, reaching into his pocket for his knife and slipping it through the knot to turn it and make a tourniquet. "Now pile onto your jughead and ride for town," he said. "I'll attend to these two."

The hateful glitter in Irick's black eyes focused on Corliss as his rage took hold of him once more. He breathed: "Give me your gun, Hal. I'll blow the damned little maverick's head off."

But Corliss pushed him roughly away, growling: "Let him alone. You got Overton and that's all that matters. Have you gone loco, Brad? Get back, I tell you."

Irick gave in then and walked sullenly over to the chestnut. "You load that rig and haul 'em in to town, Corliss," he said. "I want the sheriff to see this."

Corliss nodded and stood there, watching Irick climb awkwardly into his saddle and ride off. When he had lost sight of his boss in the murky haze, he walked back to stoop over the boy. Something he saw made him run over to his ground-haltered gelding and lift the canteen off the saddle horn. In three minutes he had Andy Overton on his feet once more.

The boy stood staring with pain-racked eyes as Corliss lifted Joe Overton's body and laid it in the buckboard. He saw Corliss throw the dirty tarpaulin over his father—the same tarpaulin they had used to cover the hides they had taken in to town. Then Corliss came to take him by the arm and lead him over and help him up into the seat.

It took a minute longer while Corliss went back after his gelding and tied the reins to the end gate, and then they were driving away from the cutbank and the dead cow and the brown stain in the sand that was Joe Overton's blood. Andy hung his head and let the tears come.

Two hours later the weathered frame buildings of Sunrise crept out of the murky dust fog. Andy hadn't spoken once during that long ride, not caring where he was being taken. Neither had Corliss. But now, as they rattled down between the two rows of false-fronted stores, he told the boy: "This ain't my doin', kid. Brad hires me and I do what he tells me."

Andy looked up at him, sensing the apology behind the words but feeling the bitterness within him override all else, saying: "You tell Brad Irick I'll kill him someday."

Corliss nodded, answering: "I reckon I'd feel the same way. But you'd better leave this country, kid. Brad Irick's poison."

That was all that was said. Andy didn't seem to care when Corliss pulled in at the hitch rail in front of the jail and got down and took him by the arm to load him across the walk in front of Bill Hazzard's office.

Hazzard himself opened the door to let them in. There were two others in the small room. Brad Irick was one, sitting there behind the sheriff's battered oak desk with his arm in a sling and a smoldering hateful light in his black eyes as he watched the boy. Tom Holman was the other, and, because Tom had been his father's friend, Andy crossed over and stood beside him at the wall where Hazzard had tacked up his faded and dusty Reward notices.

"Lock him up," Irick said bluntly.

"You leave this to me, Brad," the sheriff answered, his thin lips drawing a tight line beneath his gray mustache. He was obviously trying to control his temper as he added: "I know what to do with him."

"He's the son of a rustler and I'm havin' him arrested," Irick said. He got up out of the swivel chair and crossed the room to stand at the door. "They've got a reform school up at High Butte. I'll see that he's sent up there."

"Do anything you damned please!" Hazzard exploded. "You usually do, Irick. I may not be able to hold you for what you did to Overton, but to me it was plain murder. Now out!"

Brad Irick stood there for long seconds, an arrogant sneer twisting his thick lips and making his face ugly. "Careful, Bill," he warned. "There's an election comin' up this fall. Remember your votes."

Tom Holman spoke then, his soft Texas drawl full of a threat that his gray eyes backed: "If Bill's badge stood for your kind of law, he'd throw it away, Irick. Supposing you make yourself scarce."

The look that Brad Irick returned him made it at once obvious that a deep hostility ran between these two; it was something that had been fed by the fires of time, not a resentment flaring from these few tense seconds. His answer, coming as it did in the face of what had happened, showed plainly where he stood with Tom Holman. He said levelly: "No one asked you to buy into this, Tom. But if you want to make anything of it, you can always find me out at my layout."

He opened the door and took his time about stepping out of it, leaving behind a pregnant silence held long after Hal Corliss had followed him. At length, Bill Hazzard stepped across and kicked the door shut, the gesture relieving his feelings enough so that he could mutter: "Now, why the hell couldn't it be him that's laying out there under that tarp?" He looked over at Andy then, a little guiltily, and, when he saw the grief written across the tanned oval of the young face, all the hardness went out of him and he told the boy: "I wish there was something I could do, son."

Tom Holman leaned over and knocked the ashes out of his pipe into the five-gallon tin can that served the lawman as a waste basket, saying to Andy: "We'd better be heading up the cañon, kid."

Andy's eyes opened wide. "You're . . . you're letting me go?"

"I reckon we are," Hazzard put in. "You go with Tom, son. He thought you might want to take your dad back home."

The boy nodded dumbly, tears coming to his eyes that were full already of an unspoken thanks to these two. They had to look away.

Holman finally broke the awkward silence: "Ride out when you get the time and take a look around, Hazzard. It's not much use in all this, but I can't afford to let that herd go without at least trying to get it back."

Andy was listening, and only then realized Tom Holman's reason for being here. He had come in to see the sheriff about the loss of his yearlings. Andy was about to speak, to tell Holman that he could help him find the stolen herd, when a thought sealed his lips. He couldn't make trouble for Big-Lip Hendricks and Harry Lemon. After all, they needed meat, and his father had kept the secret. It might be that he could find the yearlings himself, without anyone ever knowing who had taken them. He would look for them; he owed that much to Tom Holman now.

On the long ride out through the smother of dust that took them up the cañon toward the Overton shack, Andy thought about those yearlings. Tom Holman sat beside him, wordless as he drove, and with the reins dangling limply from one hand. Once the boy ventured a question: "Do you figure it was Irick that took your yearlings?"

He was watching Holman as he spoke, seeing the all-consuming hatred that lighted the man's gray eyes as he drawled his answer: "Someday we'll find out, Andy. From then on maybe there'll be a little peace in this country."

That was Holman's way; he would never speak against a man unless he was certain of what he said. But the boy was satisfied with the answer. It wouldn't hurt to let him go on thinking it was Irick. That way, he'd never suspect Big-Lip and Harry.

Andy stood in the shack's doorway, watching Holman ride away down the cañon, feeling a little proud when he thought that his father had left him this friend.

Holman had made him go in and lie down on the bed while he drove the buckboard up the sloe behind and buried what was left of Joe Overton. It had taken him the better part of two hours, and Andy had gone to sleep and wakened only after Holman had finished the job and was unhitching the team over near the lean-to.

"He's up under that tallest cedar," the rancher had told him. "Tomorrow, or whenever you feel like it, ride over to my place and I'll put you on. You're big enough to help haul water, and maybe to ride herd this fall."

Andy had thanked him, hardly daring to believe in his good luck and feeling a little ashamed of the work he could do with his undersized body and his flat muscles and his growing awkwardness. Tom Holman had a heart as big as a hay barn; he would work his guts out for him.

Here in the cañon, where the wind had less of a sweep, the air was fairly clear. He could follow Holman's receding figure until his gray gelding took him around the bend in the trail, a good quarter mile below. When he was out of sight, Andy went in to eat some cold beans and pan bread. Finished, he went out to the lean-to and took his father's scarred saddle down off the pole and carried it to the corral. It took him ten minutes to catch up the black mare and saddle her. When he left the corral, it was to ride up the cañon. Big-Lip Hendricks's place was up there.

He swung wide of Hendricks's tiny nester layout, keeping to the cedars and not coming back to the road until he was out of sight of it, above. Riding on, he put the mare into a fast walk and kept a sharp look-out down at the dusty trail. A mile of this showed him nothing, so he gave it up and rode back again. Starting once more, he went back toward Hendricks's place, leaving the trail and keeping close to the near wall of the cañon.

Then he found what he was looking for—the rounded hoof-marks of a shod horse leading up the cañon.

"He was careful," Andy mused, half aloud, speaking to the mare. "He wanted to hide this sign or he'd have taken to the road."

For an hour and a half he followed that sign. It took him nearly to the top of the cañon, nearly onto open range, before it swung off and headed down a gully that branched westward. It was harder going here, for the gully spilled directly out into the weathered, time-eroded rocky maze of the badlands. Twice he lost the sign Big-Lip's bronco had left; he went back each time and picked it up before he rode on. Finally he lost it altogether and wandered on in the general direction Hendricks had taken. Fifteen minutes later, when his hopes had fallen and he was about to give up, he saw sign off to his left, close in at the foot of a low outcropping. From there it grew gradually sharper, until he could easily follow it.

They rode pretty far in to hide 'em, he told himself. He and his father had ridden in here several times, but never this far.

He suddenly remembered what his father had once told him on one of those trips: "Somewhere down here Brad Irick hides the stuff he rustles from the outfits up above. Bill Hazzard and all the rest have tried following those herds. But they're well hid. They'll never catch Irick. He'll go on at it for a spell, and finally wind up the biggest man in this country."

These last few years, since he and his father had come here, Andy listened passively to all the talk about Brad Irick. He was too young to be much interested in a thing that didn't concern him directly. But now, what had happened this day, the things he had seen and heard of Irick gave birth to the first real hatred of his life. Someday he would be big enough and old enough to settle his score with the man.

The sun's somber light was dulling in the west, and with the knowledge that dusk was coming on, Andy thought of turning back. It was then that he heard the ring of a hoof on rock behind him, and jerked around in the saddle to flash a look behind, and riding up out of the bed of a shallow wash came two riders.

They saw him at the same instant as he spotted them—and they kicked their animals in the flanks, bent low in their saddles, and came on at him in a rush. Frantically, not knowing what he was doing or where he rode, Andy Overton beat at the mare's ribs and somehow conveyed to her his feeling of terror. She lengthened her stride into a leaping run, and he hung on grimly, not daring to look back

Crack! The brittle singing of a bullet screamed past the boy's head to add to his panic. With an awed fascination he saw sweeping toward him the angular face of a low butte. The mare took him alongside it, to its farthest edge, and he reined her around behind it and headed up a steep slope and over it and down across a shallow draw.

As the mare took him over the far lip of the draw, another shot spoke out behind—this time fainter. Hope welled up in Andy; he kicked at the mare's flanks furiously and drove on. A little farther on he drew the animal in quickly and stopped her so that he could listen. Surely, ominously he heard the pounding of hoofs behind. Once more an hysterical panic gripped him; once more he beat the old mare into her wild run and went on. He was at first thankful for the darkness, but, stopping once more, he heard again the low rattle of those hoof beats.

The night was a never-ending torture, an eerie, wild dream that was to haunt him for the rest of his life. He headed always into the west, having once tried to swing back in the direction of the cañon, only to hear ahead of him that ever-present sound of the men who hunted him.

Slowly the mare began to falter, until she no longer responded to his weak attempts to keep her in her canter. With the stars blanketed out by the dust, with no moon to relieve the dense cobalt shadows, Andy Overton's terror became a thing that numbed him because he couldn't see, because he knew that at any moment the two behind might overtake him.

Exhaustion finally crept in upon him until he dozed in the saddle. He tried to fight it, but pain and grief and terror were too much against his will, and he finally gave way to sleep, clinging grimly to the saddle horn. He slept fitfully, never enough awake to be aware of the things about him, yet always fighting against his exhaustion.

He awoke with a start to look into the graying light of dawn. The thing that wakened him was the mare's abrupt breaking from her walk into a quick trot. He sawed at the reins at first, seeing her prick her ears forward and head up a slight incline that ran between two piled-up rock masses. He pulled her to a stop, and sat there for a few minutes, listening.

Then, far away, he heard the sounds of bawling cattle. He felt immediately relieved; the presence of cattle here would mean that he was close to open range, for no herd drifted down into the waterless badlands.

He let the mare have her head then, knowing by her eagerness that she had scented water. She climbed the slope at a fast trot and, topping it, brought Andy into view of what lay beyond.

There, sweeping down and away from him, was a broad basin where the tufted roots of dried bunch grass gave evidence of good grazing. In the shallow bowl of the basin, and bunched around a smear of cracked, dried mud, was a herd of yearlings.

"Tom Holman's," he breathed aloud. "Here's where Harry and Big-Lip hid 'em."

He could not hold the mare now, so he let her trot on down the slope toward the herd whose plaintive bawling already told him the answer. What he found down there was nothing but a mud hole, sucked dry by the thirsty animals. They hung around it with a dumb instinctiveness that would keep them there until the last of them had died.

Pulling the mare's head up out of the sticky ooze of mud, Andy let his glance run around the basin. It was brown and barren now, a sandy waste, but his knowledge of this country told him that here there had been good grass. At that instant he saw, far up on the opposite slope, a small shack that backed against the precipitous face of a high rocky ledge.

Someone lives here, he told himself. He kicked the mare's flanks and rode on across and climbed toward the shack.

But drawing near to it, he saw no signs of life. A nester would have put up a corral, a lean-to for a wagon. The shack was built on the wrong side of the draw for a man who had built it as a home, for up here the soil gave out and the ground was rocky and barren of growth.

Andy came down out of the saddle close in at one side of the shack. He dropped the mare's reins and went around to the door, only to find it padlocked. Then he came back to the side where he had left the mare, and stood on tiptoe to look in through the one dirty window. Inside, the gloom was unbroken by any other opening. Andy wiped the dust off the pane of glass and looked in again.

The light that filtered in through that window cast a hazy rectangle at the base of the opposite wall. There, lying on its side on the floor, was a rusty branding iron. Its grotesque pattern shaped the zigzag line of the Hacksaw, Brad Irick's brand.

"His hide-out," Andy breathed aloud, terrified at the sound of his own voice. His fear of the night was with him once more. What if those two had followed him here? What if they were Brad Irick's riders? Who else could they be, to have shot at him?

That one thought sent him over to the mare once more. As he came up to her, he saw her head come up, ears stand forward in a quick show of alarm. Looking out across the draw, Andy saw two riders walking their horses down toward the herd. They weren't looking his way.

He clamped a hand over the mare's nostrils to keep her from nickering, and then looked quickly about him for a place to hide. Off to the left a clump of piñon grew low down against the face of the ledge.

That would have to do. Paralyzed with fear, his gaze was held fascinated on the two riders below as he led the mare over to the piñon cluster. Mercifully he discovered that a shallow cleft in the rocky wall behind the piñon was large enough to hide both himself and his animal.

The minutes dragged on endlessly as Andy watched below, praying that the two would not ride up to the shack. But his hopes were soon blasted for the two riders, having ridden once around the small herd down there, headed up toward the shack at a fast trot.

When they had dismounted before the shack and crossed to the door, Andy heard one of them say: "His bronc's tracks is down there, but he's miles away by now. We'd better get on back to the layout and tell Brad."

"I'm goin' to bust open this hasp and get me a can of beans," the other answered gruffly. "Hell, we ain't had a bite since yesterday noon. All because of you wantin' to chase that damned kid."

"But what if he'd get back an' tell about what he'd found?" the other asked.

"What if he did? We didn't steal that herd. There's nothin' here to give us away."

"There's the irons inside."

"Then we'll take 'em back to the layout with us and burn this place down," the first one said. "Anyhow, there ain't a man in this country can ride in here and find the place. The kid stumbled across it. It's twenty miles to the nearest outfit, Holman's. You got the buck fever, Orlie?"

"Buck fever, hell," Orlie blustered. "I'm usin' my noodle." He stood there, watching while his partner broke the hasp with a heavy rock and swung open the door. Then he said: "You git them two cans of beans and those irons and I'll start the fire. We can use them old blankets on the bunk. There's wood by the stove, too."

It was thirty minutes before they left—thirty minutes that robbed Andy Overton of his remaining strength. He wondered at first why they hadn't looked for him, but then realized suddenly that the ground around the shack was all rock, that there was nothing to show them his sign.

"There won't be nothin' left but the stove," Orlie said, as he stood watching the smoke billow out the door from the fire he had started. "If the sheriff can make anything of that, he's welcome to it. Now let's git out of here. Bust open them cans and we'll eat as we ride."

Andy didn't move, didn't take his hands from the mare's nose, until the two had ridden out of sight over the far rim of the basin.

Then he went up into his saddle, leaving the blazing shack quickly behind, and rode into the dust-dulled glare of the sun, knowing that it would take him all day to ride to Holman's.

He was awake when the mare broke out of her walk into a trot and picked her way down into the cañon. He marked the spot with sleep-ridden eyes, seeing that it was far down toward the mouth of the cañon, below the Pinnacle Rocks that thrust their gaunt fingers up into the hazy blue of the sky that was fast losing light with the settling dusk. Behind him lay the badlands; he was dumbly thankful that that was over.

Sleep was the thing he fought against for those last three miles; his hunger and exhaustion were secondary as he swung the mare into the trail and kicked her flanks to urge her on. He rode through the thickening shadows, going blindly over a trail that was as familiar to him as the back of his hand.

All the tension went out of him as he rode past the Circle H wagon shed, nearly an hour later. His slight body was weaving in the saddle when Tom Holman himself ran out from the bunkhouse and caught the mare and lifted him to the ground.

Andy started to speak, but Tom, sensing what was wrong, cut in on his words: "It'll keep, Andy. You come on in and get some food in you."

"But I found your herd," Andy protested. "I can take you to it."

"Afterward," Tom told him. He nodded curtly to one of his riders, who immediately ran down to the cook shanty,

It was twenty minutes later—after Tom Holman had made him drink two cups of coffee and eat the biscuits and the steak and potatoes—that Andy told his story—all that his father had told him, and all that he had found out. He had decided by this time that his loyalty to Holman transcended any he owed to Big-Lip and Harry Lemon.

When he was finished, Tom said: "We'll act like we didn't know about Harry Lemon and Big-Lip Hendricks." He paused to look around the circle of faces that ringed the table. "Do you all get it? So far as we know, Brad Irick's bunch lifted that herd and drove it in there."

Holman got up from where he was sitting then. He went out the door without a word. In two minutes he was back again, with a Colt .45 in a holster hanging low at his thigh.

He looked over the group standing around Andy at the table. "Weston, you and Hip Tyler get your guns and come with me."

"I . . . I'd better go, too," Andy put in.

Holman didn't question that; he merely nodded.

But one of the others said: "Let's all ride over to the Hacksaw, Tom. You're liable to be stepping into a bear trap."

Tom Holman shook his head. "No. Brad Irick will be at his place with his sore arm. Maybe one or two others'll be there with him. The rest are out doing what you'll be doing . . . hauling water. Now get out and give those critters up in the north pasture a drink. You'll finish by midnight. Sleep in the line shack tonight and come down at sunup."

They protested at that, but Holman wouldn't budge from his decision. At length they filed out through the bunkhouse door a little reluctantly, sensing that the one thing they had been longing for was going to happen tonight, and they were to miss it. To a man, they had believed in Brad Irick's guilt, and hated him.

Weston and Hip Tyler were waiting out front with four saddled broncos when Andy and Tom Holman went out. Both of them wore six-guns strapped at their thighs. Andy felt better now; food was what he had needed most—food and the quieting presence of a man like Tom Holman.

They got into their saddles without a word and left the layout. The animal Andy rode was a bay gelding, past his prime and with a sure easy gait. They didn't ride fast, Holman seeming to sense that hurry wouldn't help things, and the others realizing it, too.

It was six miles northwest to the Hacksaw fence. Hip Tyler had a pair of wire-cutters in his pocket, and got down and clipped the four strands of the fence without having to be told to do it.

It was there that Tom Holman said: "We'll take him in to Bill Hazzard. No gun play unless he forces it."

Twenty minutes later they made out the light from a window of the Hacksaw house. By the time they saw it through the blur of the darkness and the dusk, they were in close.

That light was from Irick's office. They got out of their saddles and were crossing to the porch just as the office door swung open and outlined Brad Irick's stocky figure in the doorway. He stepped out onto the porch and into the shadow, but their eyes, accustomed to the darkness, easily followed him and picked out the details. Irick's right arm was still in its sling.

Tom and Hip Tyler led the way to the foot of the steps, with Andy hanging back a little behind Weston.

Irick looked down at the boy, then at Tom Holman and said: "You are buyin' into this, after all?"

Tom Holman nodded, taking time over his answer: "We just heard about your shack out in the breaks, Irick."

A man could have counted to ten, slowly, before Irick said: "What shack?"

"You wouldn't know, would you?" Holman drawled. "The one with irons in it. The one down in the draw where Andy found my fifty head of yearlings this morning."

"Don't run a sandy like that, Holman!" Irick exploded. "We haven't been down there. . . ." He caught himself, seeing instantly that his carelessness had given Holman the answer he needed.

"You're riding in with us to see Bill Hazzard, Irick," Holman said, his gaze fixed on the other.

Brad Irick shrugged his thickly muscled shoulders, answering: "I won't mind ridin' in to see the law. You don't have a thing on me." His left hand came up to touch the sling that encircled his right arm, and he added: "If it wasn't for this, you'd have a hard time takin' me, Tom."

Then with the quickness of a striking hawk, his left hand darted in under the sling and brought out a gun—the same horn-handled Colt that had sent Joe Overton to his death the day before.

There was nothing they could do. Tom Holman had acted instinctively, his right hand flashing to the holstered weapon at his thigh, but he was too late, and he arrested the motion.

Irick snarled: "You, kid! Step up here!"

Andy was standing at the foot of the steps, his heavy-lidded eyes wide with disbelief now at the quickness of the thing he had just seen and heard. Hesitantly he climbed the steps and crossed the park porch to where Brad Irick was standing.

"Step in front of me," Irick said smoothly, his broad face set in an arrogant smile.

But at that moment Andy Overton lunged forward and struck at the gun with his small fist. Brad Irick had been watching the others, never expecting this to happen, not knowing that the boy's exhaustion and grief had made him half crazed at the sight of his father's murderer.

Irick was quick, clubbing down a blow that caught Andy above the temple. But Tom Holman was quicker. Frantically Irick tried to raise his weapon up again after that blow. And then the tight arc of his heavy upswinging six-gun was suddenly ended as Holman's .45 exploded in a purple flame stab.

The shock of that lead slug beat Brad Irick's thick bulk back against the door frame. His brief wide-eyed stare of amazement was overridden by a gleam of fury that settled in his black eyes as they showed in the lamplight from the office. With superhuman strength, he lifted his weapon again.

Once more Holman's gun blasted the silence, and a blue hole centered itself on Brad Irick's forehead. The man's knees gave way and he slid to the board floor, his head falling loosely on his chest as he sat there with his back to the wall.

Hoarse shouts sounded up from below, by the bunkhouse.

Holman and Weston and Tyler heard them and were ready when four figures ran up out of the darkness. Those four saw the three rock-steady guns lined at them and raised their hands. One of these was Hal Corliss. He stepped in nearer, and glanced beyond Tom Holman and the others to see Brad Irick's huddled bulk against the wall.

He smiled with grim satisfaction, saying: "I reckon that needed doing, Tom."

But when Holman stepped over to kneel beside Andy Overton's still body, Corliss's smile vanished. He came up onto the porch, unmindful of the guns that menaced him, and stood there, gazing down while Holman looked at the blood smear above Andy's right ear and then felt of his chest.

"Alive?" he asked.

Tom Holman nodded, all the hardness disappearing from his face.

★ ★ ★ ★ ★

AMATEUR GUN GUARD

★ ★ ★ ★ ★

By the end of 1937, Jon Glidden's stories were selling to the better-paying Western magazines. This story, titled by the author "Death Sides a Gun-Cub", was submitted to *Dime Western* on July 25, 1937, was sold almost immediately, and the author was paid $99.00. It appeared in the November, 1937 issue under the title "Amateur Gun-Guard", which title has been retained for its inclusion here.

I

Big Ed was losing. He had lost from the beginning. He sat with his huge frame loosely slouched in his chair, a set scowl on his face, and his slitted eyes red-rimmed in the glow of the green-shaded lamp. Two empty pint whiskey bottles lay at his elbow on the table's green padding, and now, as Dave Winlay tossed in three blue chips for a raise, Big Ed straightened and sent the two bottles crashing to the floor with a single, angry sweep of his big fist.

"I'll call that," he growled, fingering his last two blues and finally tossing them to the table's center.

Dave Winlay's lean, bronzed face lost none of its impassivity as he spread his cards out fanwise on the table before him. Three jacks, and a pair of fours.

For seconds Big Ed surveyed Winlay with a deep-rooted hatred showing in his liquor-dulled glance. Those who watched, particularly Julio Sena, Big Ed's hardcase half-breed partner, waited for the explosion.

It never came. Big Ed tossed his cards face down to the discard, and muttered: "That cleans me."

The few men who stood at the bar, well away from the table, caught the reasoning behind Big Ed's action. No man in the Powder Bend country had ever before stood up to him, but this Dave Winlay was different. He had played methodically since the beginning, never giving way to Big Ed's bluffing, apparently unconcerned over his run of luck.

He was tall, yet half a head shorter than the bigger man, and he lacked forty pounds of matching the other's weight. That counted for something, yet the look in this Winlay's gray eyes, his ease of manner, and the way he wore his twin Colt .44s gave the subtle impression that here was a man well able to take care of himself.

Big Ed had spotted Winlay the day of his arrival, over three weeks ago, and it was a sure thing that sooner or later the bully would have it out with the newcomer, but so far Big Ed had failed to crack this stranger's shell of unconcern. He hadn't made up his mind about him.

"That cleans me," Big Ed said again.

Winlay greeted the remark with a shrug of the shoulders, as though the affair was settled, and began counting his winnings. Julio Sena had stood behind his boss for the past three hours and for a moment he let his dark, usually inscrutable face show his surprise. Sena had the mark of viciousness about him; he was spare-framed and wiry, and he wore his holsters tied low at his slim thighs and his two hands were soft-looking and supple, a gunman's hands.

Just now Julio bent down and whispered something to his boss. As he straightened once more, a cunning light crept into Big Ed's eyes and he stretched out a hand to cover the pile of chips at the table's center, saying thickly: "Hold on. I'm not cleaned. There's the Kid."

"The Kid?" Dave Winlay echoed, puzzlement touching his glance.

"Sure. He's worth a couple hundred. He's sixteen, strong for his size, and you could use him, stranger. He knows how to throw a rope and he can outride half the gents on this range. If you win him, you have an extra hand to work your homestead. We'll have one hand of cold showdown. It's my deal."

Winlay sat there for a full quarter minute without speaking.

He looked first at Julio Sena, and found no compromise in the man's face. Even so, it wasn't fear that made him drop his glance to Big Ed once more and drawl: "Where's this Kid? Let's have a look at him. This sounds interesting."

"Get him, Sena," Big Ed said, speaking out of the corner of his mouth.

Whitey Harms, foreman at the Lady Doris Mine and down for an evening's entertainment, had watched in silence since the game started. As Sena pushed from the circle at the table and disappeared through the swing doors up front, Whitey cleared his throat and observed: "I wouldn't do that, Ed. Your luck's bad."

Big Ed turned slowly and looked up at Whitey. His thick lips curled down in a smile. "Luck changes, Whitey. And a piker never wins a dollar. I'm makin' this play, and I'll back it."

Whitey lifted his shoulders in a gesture of unconcern and chewed the end of his cigar. For the interval of waiting, a full minute, the only sound that broke the utter quiet of the room was the click of Dave Winlay's chips as he let them slide from one hand to the other. The rest awaited the inevitable, knowing that Big Ed wouldn't let the Kid go, and that he was building his fight. Winlay probably knew, too, only it was his way to sit there with $700 of Big Ed's money stacked in front of him, as though he'd been playing for matches.

Sena brought the Kid in, shoving him roughly through the circle so that he stood inside the glow of lamplight across from Dave Winlay. The Kid's blue eyes held a look of haunting fear. Big Ed had lied; for a sixteen-year-old, the Kid was small and undernourished. A black bruise showed high on one cheek bone, and along the back of his neck ran a thin, white scar. Several of those who stood there remembered the day when Big Ed had whipped the Kid with a blacksnake in the street and left that mark upon him.

"I pulled him out of a Conestoga wagon twelve years ago, after the Apaches had raided a train headed for Fort Sumner," Big Ed announced. "I've raised him from a yearlin'. I say he's worth two hundred."

Anyone seeing Dave Winlay look up at the Kid right then would have detected a momentary softness in his glance. Yet the next instant his gray eyes had hardened to the coldness of winter granite.

"He's worth twice that," he drawled, counting out a big stack of blues and tossing them across to Big Ed. "Deal, friend. One hand of showdown."

Big Ed's face took on an arrogant smile. He raked in the chips and shuffled the cards. His two ham-like fists were surprisingly quick as he packed the deck and slapped it down for the cut. Wetting his thumb and forefinger, he picked up the pack once more and flicked out two cards, face up.

Then, with the speed of a professional tinhorn, he tossed out four more cards, two aces for himself and a pair of eights to Winlay. As his hand poised to fill in the hands, Dave Winlay straightened up out of his chair. One of his heavy Colts came up in a blurring, effortless draw.

The weapon was steady before Julio Sena's hand was halfway to holster. An instant later Winlay drawled: "Keep your shirts on, gents. And put the deck down, friend."

Big Ed's face flushed a deep brick-red. He started to say something, swallowed hard instead, and put the cards on the table.

"We'll have another deal," Winlay stated, his gun still lined. "Picking off the bottom doesn't go this hand." He flashed a look to one side and said softly: "Kid, you deal this time. Pick up the deck and begin."

The Kid's unsteady hand reached out and reluctantly took the cards. His eyes held a trace of terror as he looked down and met Big Ed's baleful stare. Yet something in Dave Winlay's manner gave him the assurance he needed. He quickly turned up two five-card hands. Not one pair showed, but Dave Winlay's jack high topped Big Ed's nine.

With a snarl of rage, Big Ed swept his cards to the floor and came to his feet, his hands away from his guns. One of his fists snaked out and clutched the Kid's shirt front and twisted it. Winlay watched, unmoving.

"That's the last bad luck you bring me," Big Ed rasped. He pulled the Kid toward him and gathered the muscles of his left arm for a blow. But in that split second Dave Winlay's Colt flashed up and out in a tight arc and smashed down across Big Ed's wrist.

Timed exactly with Winlay's move, Julio Sena's hand dropped to his holstered gun. Big Ed cried out in pain as Sena's weapon flicked up. Then Winlay's swung around in a sudden blasting gun thunder. The Mexican's weapon jumped and spun from his hand to the floor, and in the utter silence that followed his whimpering moan sounded loudly.

"Never prod me into that again," Winlay said in his flat-toned voice. "You two hit the trail and stay out of my way."

Effortlessly, as though to dare the pair, he dropped his Colt back into leather. For a moment those looking at Julio Sena thought they saw his left hand edge down toward his other weapon. But the sight of Dave Winlay's streaking draw had made a definite impression on the gunny. He turned and followed Big Ed toward the door, stooping to pick up his fallen six-gun by the trigger guard.

When the two disappeared, Dave Winlay looked across at the white-faced and trembling Kid. Winlay reached down and lifted a half-emptied shot glass off the table and handed it to the Kid, saying easily: "Drink this. It'll fix you up. Then let's you and me be on our way."

The watchers were silent, no single man among them willing to praise Winlay for what he had done. The man who spoke against Big Ed was asking for trouble. For years Big Ed had bullied these men; nothing could have pleased them more than the thing that had happened—but Big Ed was still alive and dangerous, and they were keeping out of it.

Even Whitey Harms was impressed. Whitey had come to this country two years ago to work for Brill Townley as foreman of the Lady Doris. With his grizzled hair and mustache, and a gaunt face with a thin, tight mouth, he had the look of having seen much of the world.

When Dave Winlay's glance shuttled over the crowd with a faint glint of amusement lurking deeply within his eyes, Whitey was the only one who didn't look away. The foreman of the Lady Doris permitted himself a thin smile, then turned and went out the doors.

Winlay picked up his winnings and took the Kid gently by the arm and led him out of the saloon.

"We'll ride double," he told the Kid. "Tomorrow I'll take the vinegar out of a white-faced gray out at the place. He'll make you a good horse."

The Kid said nothing. He climbed up ahead of Winlay and sat stiffly for the first mile of the ride that took them over the trail east out of Deepwell.

Dave Winlay understood the boy's silence and let him get over his first fears. Finally he said: "Forget that pair, Kid. From all I hear they're wild. There's talk that Big Ed is the best man on the range with a vent iron. But forget all that. From now on you're siding me. There's work to do at my new place and we'll have a real outfit soon. Tomorrow I'll ride over and get your things."

"No," the Kid said in a hushed voice. "Besides, I haven't got any things."

In those few words Dave Winlay understood what the Kid's life had been. A burning hatred for Big Ed took possession of him, and he knew then that meeting this man again would mean the death of one of them.

"We'll nail up another bunk alongside mine tomorrow," Dave said, more to put aside his thoughts of Big Ed than for any other reason.

"The barn's all right. That's where I've always slept. You got a barn, haven't you?"

Dave Winlay said softly: "I've got a barn. But you sleep in the house with me, Kid. We're partners."

II

The early morning sun played its light across the green of Dave Winlay's pasture and caught the yellow-gold of the turning aspens at the mouth of the cañon behind the cabin. The Kid was washing the sleep from his eyes at the tin basin on the bench alongside the door as he saw Dave riding past the corral. He wiped his face quickly with a towel, and looked up ashamedly as Dave swung from the saddle ten feet away.

"I overslept," he said in apology. "I didn't mean to."

Winlay smiled broadly. "There wasn't any good reason to get you up. I had a little job to do on the fence up the cañon. Are you handy at making flapjacks?"

Reassured at the absence of a reproach, the Kid grinned and said: "They didn't think much of my cooking at the other place. But I'll try."

Later, after Dave had devoured a big stack of the Kid's flapjacks, the boy took the two tin plates and cups down to the creek to wash them. As he finished his chore, he looked out across the pasture and saw two riders coming in along the trail from the cañon mouth. Filled with a sudden alarm, he ran up to the cabin and called in to Winlay.

"There's someone coming! Maybe they are after me!"

A moment later Dave emerged from the cabin doorway, swinging his two gun belts about his thighs, his jaw set as he glanced up the trail. But as he discovered the two riders, his gray eyes softened and he laughed and said: "They're not after you, Kid. It's Brill Townley and his girl, riding down from the mine."

The Kid's eyes lighted up. "Miss Doris? I know her. She gave me a book once." He sobered and added quietly: "But Big Ed took it away before I could read it."

Dave had seen these two before, had spoken with them a time or two as they rode past his place on their way down to Deepwell. He had heard the story of Brill Townley; how the man had spent years developing what appeared to be a poor mine, two miles up the cañon. As Brill's money gave out, people said that a rancher was a fool to try to take his money out of the earth when he had been born and bred to cattle raising. But one day, less than two months ago, there had come the rumor of a strike at the Lady Doris. Townley had kept his mouth shut about the change in his circumstances, but at least twenty strangers had come into Deepwell by stage and headed for the mine, and people knew what lay behind it.

Brill Townley made an impressive figure; he rode a coal-black gelding and sat in the saddle as straightly as a man half his years. His hair and mustache were grizzled, and Dave had been impressed with the kindly and honest look in his brown eyes.

But as Brill and his daughter approached, Dave's glance was upon the girl. Doris Townley had her father's brown eyes, and her finely molded features made a softer image of the elder Townley's aquiline face. Her hair was tawny, and her boyish figure had a suppleness that was good to see.

She had a smile for Winlay as he touched the brim of his Stetson and greeted them. " 'Morning. It's early for you two."

Brill Townley raised his brows in mock surprise: "Not so early." Then, as he swung down off his gelding, his face took on a serious expression and he looked past Dave to the Kid and said: "We heard what happened last night, Winlay. What you did was a fine thing. I want you to call on me if you get into trouble."

Dave said easily: "There won't be trouble."

"I hope not," Brill told him. Then, remembering the purpose of his visit, he went on: "I'm wondering if you'd take a job?"

"That depends. I have about all I can handle here at the layout."

"It won't interfere with your work here," Brill said. "I'm going to tell you something not many people know, Winlay. We've struck a rich vein up above. In fact, it's so rich I've been able to rig up my own smelter and reduce the ore to pretty clear bullion. But now the time's come when I'll have to haul the bars down to the bank at Deepwell. What I'm looking for is a good man to ride guard on the wagon. Whitey Harms came back with the story of what happened last night, and suggested my hiring you for the job. There'll be two trips and I'll pay you a hundred dollars a trip."

"Just to ride guard?"

Brill nodded. "It's worth it. Nothing is likely to happen, but I want to know I have a good man if it does."

"Sure, I'll do it. But I'd think you'd have at least a dozen men up there you could call on."

"Whitey claims he never saw a faster gun hand than yours. He says it took real shooting to knock that gun out of the Mexican's hand. You're the man I want. . . . You'll start down around ten o'clock tonight. Only six of us know about it. Myself, Doris, Whitey, the driver, you . . . and the Kid. Oh, yes, and Harvey Blair, who'll be at the bank to open the vault. I'll rest a lot easier when it's locked up."

Doris Townley had so far kept her silence. But now her look

showed her obvious relief as Dave gave his consent. "Thank you," she said. "This will be a big load off Dad's mind."

Whitey Harms carried the last blanket-wrapped bars of the yellow metal out of the darkened office, laid it with the rest in the bed of the ore wagon, and said softly: "That's all, boss."

"Get going, Frank," Brill Townley told the driver. "And don't stop for anything."

Dave Winlay sat beside the driver on the spring seat of the wagon. A shotgun rested across his knees, and, as old Frank picked up the reins and slapped the backs of the lead team to start them down the trail, his last glimpse of Brill Townley showed the man's high forehead wrinkled in a look of deep concern.

"The boss has the spooks," Frank grunted when they were well out of hearing.

Winlay made no answer. The night's darkness hung about them like a shroud, and for the first few minutes Dave sat peering into the cobalt shadows, unable to pick out many details. Finally, weary of the strain of trying to see through the blackness, he leaned against the seat back and braced himself against the lurching of the wagon over the uneven trail.

"Your eyes are good, mister," he ventured, two miles farther on. Frank was taking the two teams along at a fast clip.

"I've driven it a hundred times," was gaunt-faced Frank's reply. He leaned out to spit over the wheel, and added: "Those wheelers up front know the trail better than me. Hell, old Brill didn't need but one man along."

Hardly had his words broken off when, off to the left, the night was lighted with the flaming lance of a powder flash, and the roar of a gun blasted out above the rattle of the iron-tired wheels. Frank surged to his feet, dropped the reins, clawed at his chest, and then doubled up and toppled forward under the heels of the swing team. Dave made one frantic attempt to catch the falling man, failed, and at the last moment caught the reins as they were sliding off the seat.

The horses lunged ahead in a mad run as other shots winked out into the night. Dave hauled in on the reins, momentarily fearing what might happen if he gave the animals their heads. But then, remembering Frank's claim that the horses knew the trail better than he knew it himself, he wound the reins around the brake arm and rolled back into the wagon bed as a bullet seared his right arm.

He was none too soon, for a moment later hard-riding horseman came pounding up out of the darkness behind and emptied a six-gun pointblank at the wagon.

Dave crouched lower behind the protection of the thick plank siding. Bullets whipped into the planking and cut the air above his head. As the fifth rocketing blast of that six-gun beat the air, he came to his knees, swung the shotgun to his shoulder, and squeezed both triggers. A lurch of the wagon spoiled his accurate aim, yet on the heel of the double concussion he heard a cry of pain and saw the shadow behind swing to one side. Then the massive bulk of the rider pitched from the saddle to the side of the trail.

There was within him almost a certainty that the rider's burly figure was that of Big Ed. His men, it must have been, who were out there in the night. Julio Sena would be there, too, perhaps one or two more hardcases.

Dave's thoughts went back to the Kid, alone in the cabin tonight. He wondered if the Kid would be safe, and promised himself to give the boy a gun tomorrow.

Time and again he rose up and emptied his guns at those faint shadows behind. Once he thought he heard another cry, far behind, but he could not be sure. Soon afterward the hoof pound of the pursuing horsemen faded out, and only the rattle of the wagon wheels and the creak of harness and the hoof clatter of the two teams ahead came to his ears. In another half minute he lifted himself up and into the seat. A quarter mile farther on and he had the teams in check, letting them go on at a fast trot.

At the bank, Harvey Blair listened to his story. In grim silence the banker helped unload the heavy yellow bars and carry them into the vault, where he swung shut and locked the massive door.

"You'd better come along with me and see the sheriff about this," he told Dave. "He ought to know. We'll probably find him at home in bed."

It was past midnight when they started up the street to the sheriff's house that lay at the east end of town. Dave had told Blair only the simple facts of the attempted robbery; he had mentioned no names and offered no opinions.

It was surprising now to hear Blair say: "There's only one jasper in this country who'd try a thing like that, and I'm speaking of Big Ed. If we had more like you here, Winlay, we'd rare up on our hind legs and run him off this range."

Dave was about to reply, when Blair suddenly reached out, grasped his arm, and pulled him to a stop. Two hundred yards ahead, at the town's far limits, the trail in from the east ran for several rods over bare rock, and now they heard the rattle of iron tires on that stretch of rock, and the unmistakable pounding of iron-shod hoofs as a team came toward them at a fast clip.

"It's late, and that gent's in a big hurry," Blair muttered. "We'll wait right here and see who it is."

This was no idle curiosity on the banker's part. It was odd for anyone to be driving into town at this time of night, stranger yet that whoever it was should be in such a hurry.

There was a five-second wait and then, from out of the half-lighted distance, appeared a team pulling a light buckboard. At the moment they came into sight the animals slowed to a trot and wheeled in toward the walk. And then Harvey Blair was breathing—"Brill Townley."—and Dave Winlay recognized the mine owner on the driver's seat of the buckboard.

"He's turned in at the sheriff's house!" Blair shouted, starting off down the walk at a run with Dave following closely behind. Before they had drawn abreast of the buckboard, they saw two other figures climb out of the shallow bed of the vehicle and help down a third man, a big man.

It was Big Ed, his arms laced behind him and held on either side by one of Brill Townley's crew from the mine.

Townley heard Blair and Dave approaching along the boardwalk and hesitated in climbing down from his seat. Then, seeing who it was, he jumped to the ground and said: "God Almighty, I'm glad to see you, Winlay. Is the gold safe?"

"As safe as it'll ever be," Blair put in, regarding Big Ed with a hard glance. "Where did you find this chunk of hang-noose meat, Townley?"

"We heard the shooting up at the mine and drove down to see what it was. Big Ed was lying in the trail. One of your slugs caught him in the shoulder, Winlay, and knocked him out of the saddle. He hit his head on a rock as he landed."

"What about Frank?" Dave asked.

In answer, Brill Townley shook his grizzled head soberly. A sudden rising anger sent Dave up the walk until he stood face to face with Big Ed. He had to fight back the impulse to strike the man.

Big Ed's face was a dirty yellow, his shoulders and left sleeve were smeared with blood, and he stood weakly on his two unsteady legs. There was no fight left in him.

Winlay turned back to the others, disgust showing clearly on his lean face: "What're we waiting for?" he asked flatly. "Let's get this over with."

They roused Sheriff Ransom, and he went with them down the street and opened up the jail. Big Ed was locked in one of the three cells, charged with attempted robbery and first-degree murder. Harvey Blair left soon afterward, promising to stop at the doctor's house on the way home and send the sawbones back to patch Big Ed's wounded shoulder.

Before Brill Townley left Deepwell that night he had posted rewards for the apprehension of Julio Sena, and the sheriff had started the job of gathering a posse to ride with him up Timber Gulch to Big Ed's cabin.

Brill Townley directed his two men to go down to the bank after his wagon and drive it back to the mine. He and Dave started ahead in the buckboard.

The mine owner was silent for the first part of their two-hour ride. But when they rounded the bend in the trail and headed for Dave's layout, he spoke suddenly.

"You made a real job of it, Winlay, and you have my thanks. But it may mean that we'll have trouble on the second trip. Julio Sena isn't through in this country. Neither is the man who's workin' with him and Big Ed."

"Who would that be?" Dave queried, puzzled at the meaning behind the words.

"I told you this morning that only a half dozen of us knew the gold was being brought down. There's a leak somewhere. Big Ed got to my men in some way and learned about our plans."

"Could it be Whitey Harms?"

Brill Townley shook his head. "Whitey has worked for me for years. He's to be trusted. No, Big Ed got his information some other way."

"What about the second trip? Do you still want me to try it?"

Townley nodded. "I don't have any choice. The safe in my office isn't any too strong, and we'd better get the rest of it down to the bank. With Sena on the loose, there's no telling what'll happen." He paused, looking up at Dave, and said finally: "There's no need in your riding guard again tonight if you choose not to. I can get another man."

"I wouldn't sell my seat on that wagon for double what you're paying me," Dave told him. "Count me in on it. Only, if I were you, I'd put more than one guard on this trip."

"I'll send Harms along. He can drive," Townley said.

As they rode on, Dave Winlay considered the thing. He didn't know anything against Whitey Harms, but he couldn't put from his mind the fact that someone Townley had trusted had told Big Ed about the trip down to the bank. . . .

III

The Kid asked in a small voice: "Then he's in prison? Will they hang him?"

Dave Winlay hid his surprise at the boy's concern and said easily: "No, I don't reckon they will. There's no proof that Big Ed was the one who shot Frank. They'll probably send him to Yuma for a few years. Now let's forget this and go out after that gray I promised you."

The Kid followed Winlay down to the corral and watched him saddle the palomino. He was plainly worried, for now that Big Ed was in trouble he momentarily forgot the treatment he had been given for the past twelve years. On the ride up the pasture he was unusually quiet. It wasn't until Dave had spied the gray that the Kid forgot his troubles.

Dave set the Kid down and went after the gray; in five minutes he had a rope on the animal. For the next half hour the Kid stood fascinated, watching Dave take the wildness out of the gray. Finally Dave rode up and dismounted.

"He's ready," he told the Kid. "Climb up and try him."

For the first half minute the Kid forgot the things Big Ed had taught him about riding, and the gray's nervousness was magnified a hundred times in the weaving saddle. But then, as quickly as it had come, the Kid's nervousness left him; he settled down in leather and let the animal break out into a stretching run. They went the whole two mile length of the pasture, Dave following on the palomino. And, when the Kid easily checked the horse at the cedars before the cañon mouth, his smooth young face was set in a broad smile. The gray was his.

"There's something else," Dave announced. "Ride on back to the cabin and I'll show you." He wheeled with the Kid.

They ground-haltered the horses in the yard, and Dave led the way inside. He went to his bunk and stooped down to pull out a heavy leather bag. Opening the flap, he rummaged inside for a moment and finally lifted out a worn but well-oiled Colt .38 and an old plain leather holster and shell belt with a few of the loops torn loose. He held it out to the Kid, along with a box of shells.

"It's yours, Kid."

The boy's eyes widened. Hesitantly his hand reached out and he took the weapon and turned it over and over, carefully, as though handling something that might be broken at touch. He stammered: "It's . . . it's a real one. I never . . . never had one before. Gee, thanks."

"We'll punch a new hole in the belt," Dave said, taking out his knife and working the point of the blade through the belt leather. Then, strapping it around the Kid's waist, he added: "That's to use, Kid . . . if you ever need it."

The words sobered the boy. He asked Dave: "When would I ever need it?"

Dave shrugged his wide shoulders. "Probably never. Let's hope you won't. But you ought to know how to get it out and how to aim it if the time ever comes. Practice never hurt anybody."

The Kid thought about that. After the noon meal he belted on his six-gun and announced to Dave that he was taking the gray out for a workout.

"Ride north up the cañon," was Dave's only suggestion. He gave it casually, but the Kid understood. Big Ed's cabin lay below, and it wasn't hard to guess that Dave was thinking of Julio Sena, thinking that he might be in hiding near there.

The Kid climbed into the saddle and headed up the pasture and into the narrower limits of the cañon. He felt very happy. In the past he had experienced rare moments of happiness, such as the time Doris Townley had given him that book; now, to realize that Dave Winlay was his friend brought on an emotional uplift that numbed him.

It happened suddenly, so quickly that it was like a hard blow in the Kid's face. He was skirting a belt of cedar when Julio Sena suddenly prodded his roan mare out from the shelter of the trees and blocked the trail.

The Kid jerked in on the reins and the gray shied, reared on hind legs, and finally quieted to a prancing nervousness.

Julio rode in close, his face masked in that inscrutability that the Kid knew so well. The Mexican's eye ran over the gray horse, picked out the Kid's holstered six-gun. He said silkily: "You do well, Keed. A horse, a gun . . . and a *gringo* friend."

For the first time the Kid thought of his gun, at the same time knowing that it would be suicide to let his hand get anywhere near it. A flash of movement beyond Julio caught his eye, and, looking over toward the trees, he saw Whitey Harms reining his bronco out into the trail.

"What are you doing here?" the Kid queried, knowing before he asked the question that Whitey Harms was the one who had betrayed Brill Townley.

Harms's glance remained impassive as he drawled: "Let Sena tell you, Kid."

Sena nodded. "Yes, I tell you. You hear about Beeg Ed?"

The Kid waited silently.

"Don't be afraid," Julio went on. "We come to you for help."

"To me for help?" the Kid echoed.

Julio gave another slow nod. "We ride for the border tonight, Keed. We want to take Beeg Ed along."

"But he's in jail."

Julio shrugged and let his face take on a sober, half-wistful expression. "That's the trouble. Whitey think maybe you help us. I tell him no. I say you hate beeg Ed. You glad he's in prison."

The Kid caught a hint of what was coming, and with the knowledge of what Julio was suggesting the old haunting fear once more rode through him.

Julio reached into a pocket of his waist overalls and pulled out a big key and held it up before him, his hand relaxed. "Thees key, she open Beeg Ed's cell. He could walk out free man if he had it. Whitey say for you to take it to Beeg Ed, I say no, you won't, because you hate him. An' me . . . I am what you call not so welcome in town, no?"

The Kid, his gaze fascinated by the key, breathed: "He deserves what he's getting. He'll be in prison for years."

Julio nodded. "That is right. But what happen when he get out, Keed? He hunt you down. Maybe keel you."

Sena had timed his threat perfectly. Knowing that he alone could secure Big Ed's freedom, the Kid was terrified. He knew Sena, knew of the man's merciless cunning, and there was little doubt of what was to come. If he escaped Sena, Big Ed would find out that he had refused to give him his freedom. Years from now, even if he rode far from this country, Big Ed would hunt him down.

"Beeg Ed, he raise you from a little one," Sena was saying.

"He take you from the Apaches and save your life, Keed. If you take him this key, he ride with me for the border tonight. You stay here and live with *Señor* Winlay, but we go." He paused a moment, waiting for the words to take effect. Then: "I tell Whitey it no good. You no do this for Beeg Ed."

A frenzy of thought bewildered the Kid. It was as Julio had said; he did owe Big Ed his life. If he took that key, took it in to Big Ed, these two would forever pass from his life. That way he could live in peace with Dave Winlay. On the other hand, if Big Ed ever learned that the Kid had refused the chance of giving him his freedom, he would someday hunt him down for a reckoning. The Kid trembled with the picture of what would happen. Big Ed would break him in his two big hands; the man had no mercy for him.

Slowly, against his will, he reached out a hand and took that key. The touch of the cold steel sent a shiver coursing along his spine, made him realize that he was betraying Dave Winlay's trust in him. But the inbred fear of a dozen agonizing years was too strong for the weight of this newfound friendship; anyway, he was getting Big Ed out of the way for good, even though he didn't go to prison. This was the only way out for him.

He pocketed the key, wheeled the gray, and started slowly back along the trail. As he rode away, he heard Sena say: "Go to the jail right after dark. Tell Ed we wait for him by Five Mile Rock."

For an instant, tight-lipped, the Kid thought again of Dave Winlay. He'd understand; he'd help him find a way out. But Winlay was already at the mine, and now it would be too late to get him before he started for town. No, the best way, the surest way of clearing up the whole thing and making the future safe both for Winlay and himself was to go into town and give Big Ed that key. His shoulders drooped as he headed the gray toward Deepwell.

IV

A mile short of town he reined in on the gray and spent two minutes rolling his belt and gun in his slicker behind the saddle. He handled the weapon fondly, for the feel of it brought up a clear image of Dave Winlay in his mind. Then, hating himself for what he was doing, he rode on, straight down the middle of Deepwell's broad and rutted street. He swung in at the tie rail in front of the jail, noted the guard standing at the far end of the building with a rifle in the crook of his arm, and went across the walk and into Sheriff Hugh Ransom's lighted office.

" 'Evening, son," was the lawman's greeting. He sat behind a table. "What can I do for you?"

The Kid shifted nervously from one foot to the other. "Can I see Big Ed?"

"Sure," was Ransom's cordial response. "Just so you don't pass him a gun, or a file, or anything he could use to break out with." He caught the Kid's startled look and broke out into a hearty laugh. "Come on. I'll unlock the door for you."

As he swung back the steel-faced cell-block door, he added: "Take all the time you want, son."

Then he was looking through the bars at Big Ed's massive figure lying on a dirty cot in the middle cell. The man stirred and pushed himself up onto one elbow and looked out at the boy. His beard-stubbled face broke into a sneering smile, and he grunted: "Damned if I expected to ever see you again, maverick. What the hell do you want?"

The Kid stepped forward reluctantly and reached into his pocket and pulled out the key. Big Ed's glance dropped to discover the key, and with sight of it his eyes widened and then narrowed in a look of cunning. He jumped up and came to the barred door of the cell and held out his hand, snarling: "Give it here. All hell couldn't keep me in this place another hour."

But the Kid held back. "You're to meet Julio out at Five Mile

Rock," he said, his voice barely above a whisper. "He said you were riding for the border tonight. Promise me you'll not come back?"

Ed's barrel chest heaved in a low chuckle. "Promise? Sure, I'll promise anything, Kid. Only hand over that key."

"You're not to kill anyone getting out of here." The Kid tendered the key. "Remember . . . you've promised never to come back."

Big Ed took the key, flashed a look at the door, and snarled: "Why would I ever come back? For you? The best that ever happened to me was for Winlay to take you off my hands. Beat it, Kid. Things'll start happenin' in a minute."

Now that this was over, a trembling weakness hit the Kid. He turned and went out through the office, not trusting himself to look at the sheriff.

As he mounted and headed back down the street, his body was bathed in an icy perspiration, yet he felt an exhilaration he had never before experienced. Big Ed was gone, forever!

He was less than a quarter of a mile beyond the town's limits when he heard the staccato bark of a six-gun crash in the distance behind. He sawed on the reins, brought the gray to a standstill, and waited, listening tensely.

He faintly heard voices shouting back there along the street. Then, ten seconds later, he heard the low throb of pounding hoofs; they grew louder, and in sudden alarm he wheeled the gray around and streaked off down the trail.

Twice he stopped, and heard the hoof throb of that oncoming rider, closer each time. He had no illusions now. In some way Big Ed had found a gun—probably he'd taken it from the unsuspecting Hugh Ransom—and he had shot his way free, stolen a horse, and was now headed for Five Mile Rock.

He realized this only as towering Five Mile Rock loomed up ahead.

A sudden frenzy made him swerve off the trail with the intention of cutting a wide circle around the rock. Julio Sena would be waiting there, and he had no wish to meet him. He headed the gray at a right angle to the trail.

Suddenly, out of the gloom ahead, loomed a horseman. The Kid slid the gray to a halt, but he was too late. Before he could turn the animal and ride away, Julio Sena had come up out of the darkness and was sitting in his saddle twenty feet way, the nickeled barrel of his six-gun glinting softly in his hand.

"Don't go, Keed!" Sena called out. "Did you take Beeg Ed the key?"

The Kid swallowed with difficulty and answered: "He has it. Let me go!"

Sena smiled thinly. "You stay weeth me, *chopito!* We wait for Beeg Ed."

At that moment, far back along the trail they heard that hoof pound that had haunted the Kid on his long ride.

"That must be him now," Sena muttered. "Turn around, Keed, and head for the trail. And no funny beesness. My finger itch to pull thees trigger."

It was Big Ed. He had two six-guns stuck through the waistband of his Levi's; the sling around his right arm was red with matted blood. He was breathing hard, and the animal he rode, a slim-legged chestnut, was badly blown.

"They're after me," Big Ed breathed, as soon as Julio had ridden alongside him. "Let's ride. We can be across the border by daybreak."

"You forget sometheeng," Julio put in. "The gold. Whitey drives it down tonight. *El Señor* Winlay is with him. We take thees trail on up to meet them. The posse, she think we head south. We got plenty time to ride to border."

The Kid heard, and, before Julio had finished speaking, he was wheeling the gray around in a rearing plunge off into the shadows alongside the trail.

The Mexican's hand flashed up in a bursting lance of gun flame, but the Kid, bending low over the gray's neck, made an indistinct target, and a second later had put the shadow of a stunted piñon between him and the gunny.

He had a five second start, that only, for on the heel of that single gun blast he heard the booming of hoofs ring out behind. Big Ed and Sena plunged off the trail, hot on the heels of the gray.

In the first quarter mile, Sena took deliberate aim and emptied his gun at the Kid. But at this terrific pace no man could have sent a bullet true. It settled down to a grim race with death, the Kid swerving from time to time as he heard the two behind drawing nearer.

The Kid swung into the cañon trail and scant seconds later Big Ed and Sena hit the trail behind him. Big Ed fell behind a little, but Sena slowly closed the gap that separated him from the Kid. Slowly the drum of the bay's iron-shod hoofs sounded out above the clatter of the gray's beating run, until the Kid looked back and saw the spare-framed half-breed gunman a scant fifty yards to his rear.

Then from out of the hazy night the Kid saw an indistinct shape ride up out of the gray ribbon of the trail toward him. He watched it with a growing fascination until at last a cry of joy and relief broke from his lips.

"Dave!" he shouted, but his words were whipped back by the wind.

Yet that cry spurred the gray on. With a last mighty surge, the animal stretched into a run that held the gap between him and the bay Julio Sena rode.

The Kid heard a faint cry up ahead, saw a figure rise up off the seat of the double-teamed wagon, and a moment later he was flashing past. In the fleeting glimpse he had, the Kid saw

Dave fall backward off the seat from the impact of Whitey Harms smashing fist.

It all came to him then. Whitey and Big Ed and Sena had framed this, framed it to make a getaway with Brill Townley's gold. It was three against one, and no man could expect to come out alive from under the guns of those three.

"But it isn't three against one," the Kid muttered, wheeling the gray about. He rammed home his spurs and headed back to the wagon, reaching back for the walnut-handled gun Dave Winlay had given him that morning.

He pulled the gun loose as he came alongside the wagon. Whitey and Dave were sprawled in the wagon bed now, on top of the blanketed bars of the precious metal, Whitey on top. It was sheer agony to the Kid to see Whitey's six-gun arc up for a smashing blow at Dave's head. Frantically the Kid swung his weapon around, and, as the gray drew alongside, the boy thumbed back the hammer and pulled the trigger of the unfamiliar weapon.

It was an impossible shot, yet as the whip of the gun threw up his small hand, the Kid saw Whitey's gaunt frame go suddenly loose. The mine foreman clawed at his chest and then fell, sprawling on top of Dave Winlay. And in the next split second the Kid felt a rushing shadow slip past him and he was blinded and deafened by the brilliance of a powder flash.

It was Julio Sena. He had ridden up at a hard run and was passing within arm's reach of the Kid. Yet, so great was the speed of the running bay, that Sena's bullet only scorched the Kid's head. He felt the pain of that bullet crease, realized suddenly that the Mexican was for the moment out of it, and looked over once more at Dave Winlay. Dave was coming to his feet now, swinging up his double-barreled shotgun.

A purple flame suddenly spurted from Dave Winlay's shotgun at the fleeting figure of Big Ed's renegade partner. Sena stood upright in his stirrups, his two hands. high above his shoulders and his head upturned as though worshipping some moon god as the double charge of buckshot whipped into him. He reeled drunkenly in the saddle of the still running bay, and a moment later the wheeling of the animal threw him out of the saddle. He lit on one shoulder, slid a few feet in the dust, and then his body pinwheeled over in a crazy, broken-boned heap.

"Watch Big Ed!" the Kid cried.

Dave Winlay had no need for that warning. He threw the empty shotgun to the bed of the wagon, and then, spraddlelegged, his two hands streaked to his twin holsters and palmed up the two .44s. Big Ed came pounding up, his horse running abreast the wheelers of the ore wagon, and then both men were emptying their guns.

Big Ed came on, his bulky body jerking crazily as Dave's slug whipped into him. He was falling sideways from the saddle, directly at the Kid. With a crushing impact, Big Ed's body swept the Kid from the saddle. A white sheet of light crossed the Kid's vision, and he knew no more. . . .

Later, the Kid opened his eyes and looked up into Doris Townley's tear-filled gaze. He was in a bed, between smooth white sheets, and the slab-walled room was strangely unfamiliar. His voice barely above a whisper, he asked: "What happened to Dave?"

"I'm here, Kid."

The Kid turned his head and saw Winlay standing at the other side of the bed. A bandage was about Dave's head and below it the man's lean face had a sober set the Kid had never before seen.

A flood of memory made the Kid suddenly push himself up in his bed. Strangly enough, he felt no pain.

Dave Winlay, seeing this, smiled and said: "That means we're both all right, Kid." He took the boy's hand in his. "If it hadn't been for you, I'd be lyin' out there on the trail, and those three would be halfway to the border."

The Kid barely heard what his friend was saying. Instead, he was remembering that he had taken Big Ed the key, that all this wouldn't have happened but for that.

"You know . . . you know what I did now, don't you?" he asked filled once more with self-hate.

Dave nodded. "We know . . . Doris and Hugh Ransom and me. Hugh just rode up here to the mine with his posse. He's got a short memory, Kid. So have I. From now on you're my kid."

"Your kid?" the boy echoed, puzzled.

Dave Winlay's face flushed a trifle, while the Kid, understanding what it meant, had a smile of happiness on his thin young face.

★ ★ ★ ★ ★

Dead Man's Assay

★ ★ ★ ★ ★

Following military service during the Second World War, Jon Glidden returned to writing Western fiction. Several of his book-length novels were serialized in *The Saturday Evening Post,* while his agent kept both him and T.T. Flynn writing short fiction for pulp magazines. "Dead Man's Assay" was sold to *Fifteen Western Tales* on September 15, 1947. The author was paid 3¢ a word, up a penny a word from what he had received before the war from Popular Publications, and the title was changed to "Dead Man's Draw" upon publication in the February, 1948 issue. The author's original title has been restored for its appearance here.

I

It finally looked like the end of an interminable wait. The teams were hitched and the driver had tossed the mail sack up into the front boot. Now he was climbing after it, the high-bodied Concord swaying gently to his weight.

Then a man in shirt sleeves, the agent, came to the lighted door of the stage office and bawled: "Hold it, Slim."

Steve Lord, sitting in the stage's back-facing seat with his shoulders hunched to make more room for the girl beside him, heard the driver curse and then call complainingly: "For the love of God, I'm already two hours late, Fred! Shake a leg or I'll. . . ."

His voice broke off as Steve Lord saw this big man come out the door past the agent onto the platform. Then the coach swayed again and the driver was aground, saying respectfully: " 'Evenin', Mister Young. Didn't know it was you."

"Hello, Slim. Hear you're full up."

"Never any other way."

The big man, Young, came on over now and looked casually in through the open door window of the coach, smiling a little when he saw how jammed in the nine passengers were. The fat drummer, sitting on the far side of the girl, complained: "Let's get started. This delay's costing me." The rest of them simply stared at Young, their looks ranging from complete boredom to impatience and even outright anger over his causing them to sit here longer.

Young turned to the driver now. "Better unload the last two that bought tickets, Slim. Two Card's with me." He had no sooner spoken than another man appeared from the stage office. This one was black-suited, a heavy gold watch chain sagging across his black and white checked vest. His gray derby was cocked at a jaunty angle and long dark sideburns heightened the pallor of his thin face.

"Howdy, Two Card," Slim drawled. Then he called: "Fred, who's the last two that bought ducats?"

The station agent thought a moment. "The girl and that cowpoke."

Steve Lord knew what was coming even as Slim opened the door and nodded to him. "Sorry, stranger, but you gotta wait for the next run. You, too, miss."

"I'm staying right where I am," said the girl quietly, only the faintest edge to her voice that Steve could tie in with her dark red hair. "I've waited two days, paid my money, and I won't give up my seat to someone who came after me."

"But, miss, this man here's. . . ."

"I don't care who he is or what he is. I'm going to Summit on this stage."

Slim was embarrassed and momentarily baffled, the color mounting to his face. He turned away and called helplessly: "Fred, come out and settle this!"

As the agent sauntered out from the office doorway, Steve was watching the faint smile playing across big Young's square-jawed face. There was something so smug and self-satisfied about the smile that now Steve added his word to the girl's. "We both go this trip, Slim."

"Now, look here," Slim had time to protest before the agent was pushing him aside and glancing in through the door.

The agent gave a curt jerk of the head. "Out, you two. This man and his friend have important business in Summit.

Furthermore, Miles Young owns this line. If anyone's got a right to a seat, he has."

"We bought our rights when we bought our tickets," the girl argued.

Young's smile broadened. He gave Slim a spare nod, drawling—"Toss down their things."—and Slim stepped out of sight, the coach shortly lurching as he climbed to the back boot. And the station man, hoping the matter settled, turned and walked back into his office.

Steve gave the girl a look. "You really want to travel up there tonight, miss?"

Her look was uncertain now. He could see that she was a little afraid. Yet she said: "I certainly do." He liked the way she tilted her head up as she spoke,

His glance went out to Young then and he caught the man's eye. "It's no go, friend. We stick."

"Two Card, you're needed here," Young said flatly, no longer smiling.

The big man's dapper companion stepped up to the door and with his left hand disarmingly lifted his hat to the girl, saying gently: "Beg your pardon, miss, but you'll have to get down." As he spoke, his right hand reached lazily in under his coat and came out fisting a pepperbox Derringer.

The surprise was quite complete and unexpected, even though Steve had been regarding Two Card closely. The snub-nosed weapon settled into line with Steve's wide chest and Two Card added, just as smoothly: "The same goes for you, sir."

There was a quality in the chill look of his gray eyes that belied the politeness of his speech. Warned by it, Steve put a tight rein on his rising anger. He eased his long length off the seat, swinging aground. It didn't help his frame of mind to remember the Colt and shell belt in his war bag, although he knew he couldn't have anticipated this unexpected circumstance.

Nothing to do about it, he told himself and, to cover his confusion, turned and offered the girl a hand. "Looks like we eat our crow and like it, miss. Can I help you down?"

He could see the delicate molding of her face set determinedly. "I'm staying right here."

"Now, miss," Two Card said, lowering the gun and letting it hang at his side as he stepped well clear of Steve, "you're only delaying things. You have our apologies, but. . . ."

"Catch, stranger!" Slim called from the roof of the coach just then. He had lifted Steve's sacked saddle from the rear boot and now swung it out toward Steve and dropped it.

"But you'll have to give up your seat," Two Card went on again to the girl, his annoyed glance shuttling briefly up to Slim.

Steve took the saddle's dropping weight easily with a pendulum-like motion that arced it down, then up again. He threw it hard.

At the last instant Two Card saw it coming and tried to dodge. But by then it was too late. The saddle caught him on the shoulder and bowled him over. He grunted with pain as his back slammed into the platform boards and he made one frantic hurried effort to lift the Derringer. But Steve, following the saddle, snatched at the weapon and twisted it from his grasp.

The Derringer rocked around to freeze the motion of Young's massive fist sweeping his coat clear of his holster. Steve drawled—"Easy now."—and stepped in behind him, relieving him of his .45.

Two Card picked himself up off the boards, beat the dust from his carefully pressed coat, and retrieved the gray derby that had rolled away. When he turned once more, Steve made a spare motion with the Derringer. "Heave it up again, fella."

Slim had been crouching motionlessly on the roof and slowly stood erect now. There was an expression of disbelief and awe on his narrow face as he looked down first at Steve, then at Young. A man inside the coach breathed delightedly: "Brother, did you see that?" A deeper voice in there snapped: "Shut up!"

Two Card was having a hard time making up his mind. Young was regarding Steve as though just seeing him for the first time. There was a cold and killing rage etched briefly on his broad face. Then he made up his mind to something and said: "Better do it, Two Card."

The saddle was a good bit heavier for Two Card than it had been for Steve. He lost most of his dignity as he picked it up and staggered under the load. In the end he was overbalanced by it and let it fall against the coach's side and Slim reached down and relieved him of it, needing no prompting from Steve to drop it into the back boot once more.

The agent, having missed all this, now came out the door once more, scanning a sheet of paper in his hand. Without looking up he called: "Mister Young, you might like to take this. . . ." Just then his glance lifted; he came to a quick halt and stood staring as though he couldn't believe his eyes.

"Let's roll, Slim," Steve drawled. He stepped lightly onto the front wheel hub and swung up onto the driver's seat, adding: "Might as well give 'em more room inside."

His glance hadn't left the two below and now he broke open the Derringer, shaking out the loads, and tossing it so that it fell at Two Card's feet. He held Young's .45 in his lap as Slim eased down to the seat beside him and, giving him a wary sideward glance, unwound the reins from the brake arm.

"Be seeing you," Steve spoke almost cheerily to the men below.

Slim booted off the brake and put his three teams into motion. Young's answer sounded over the abrupt clatter of hoofs against the hard-packed earth. "That you will, my friend."

They were better than a mile out from town and the Concord was rolling along a straight stretch of the rutted road before Slim said: "That Two Card Grant now, he's an unforgiving son-of-a-bitch. Miles Young is worse. Brother, you sure you want to go up there? Summit is Young's town."

"I heard it was a gold camp."

Slim looked sideways at Steve, trying to read his expression in the starlight, thinking: *He's a cool one.* Aloud, he said: "So it is. But Miles owns the smelter, the Crestview, the hotel, and half a dozen mines. People just don't buck him."

"They don't?"

Slim breathed a deep sigh, impressed even more by this stranger's sparseness of speech than by his looks for Steve looked like many of the breed of cowpunchers who were trying their luck up in the boom camp. He was tall, taller than most, and had that lean look of rawhide toughness that went with the high-heeled boots, the waist overalls, and the wide hat. Slim remembered how genial and harmless-looking this blond man had been back there even when he threw down on Two Card with the gambler's own gun. And now he said fervently: "Yes, sir, I'd hate to be runnin' into them two again if I was you."

"Think I'll get some shut-eye," was all Steve said. And he crawled on back and stretched out between two valises Slim had roped to the roof rails.

Slim shook his head wonderingly at the unconcern of this man who had taken out such a hefty mortgage on trouble, real trouble. Then, with nothing better to do, he lit himself a cigar and settled down to the tiresome job of driving.

The lights of their first stop, the desert station of Cinder, dropped out of sight beyond a hill behind the Concord at 2:00 that morning after Slim had harnessed a relay of fresh horses.

Steve hadn't stirred during the stop and only a couple of the others—the red-haired girl and the fat man—even got out to stretch. By the time they reached the beginning of the foothills, better than an hour later, the furnace heat of the air was thinning before a cool gentle breeze. Some two hours after that Slim swung his tired teams in on the hill station at Chimney Rock, the first gray light of dawn showing over the peaks. And he bawled as he booted home the brake: "All out, folks! Breakfast!"

The meal wasn't much, being the same as a passenger would find noon or night at this forlorn spot—boiled beef, boiled potatoes, canned tomatoes, and cold biscuits. The flies were bad and the coffee good, strong enough to jolt Steve thoroughly awake after his five solid hours of sleep.

When they filed tiredly out to the stage again, the fat drummer told Steve: "You ride inside a while. I want a look at the country."

So Steve took the seat he'd had in the beginning, the one next to the girl, and, as the light strengthened, he braced himself against the lurching of the coach and tried to make his shoulder a comfortable rest for her head after her efforts at staying awake had failed. He would look down at her now and then, and, when the others were all finally dozing, he let his glance linger.

She was something out of the ordinary for this country, for any country. She had taken off the small, flat-brimmed straw hat, and, when he lowered his head, he could catch the faint scent of a light perfume in her high-piled hair. It seemed a deeper auburn in the day's strengthening light than it had last night in the lamplight back there in town. She was even prettier than he had first thought. Instead of the light skin of most women with that hair, hers showed a deeper tone, a creaminess that gave her good looks added depth and a certain subtlety. She had somehow managed to keep herself well-groomed and clean-looking over this long and dusty ride and he wondered now that no tiredness showed in her face.

He was thinking these things when she opened her eyes quite suddenly, looking directly up at him. She stayed as she was a long moment, close to him and her head nestled to his shoulder. Then a smile touched her eyes and she straightened, saying: "You should have wakened me. Your shoulder must be numb."

"Far from it." He grinned broadly. "Isn't often this shoulder gets a chance at such a pleasant chore, miss."

She laughed softly, merrily and reached up and straightened her hair, although there was no need for it. Once more she looked across at him. "I haven't yet thanked you for seeing they didn't put me off back there."

"That was a close one."

"Those men were quite angry with you."

"They'll get over it."

She gave him an odd speculative glance. "You don't seem to be worrying. I heard some of what the driver said."

Steve shrugged and, slightly ill at ease, reached to a shirt pocket and took out a sack of tobacco. Then he thought better of it and was returning the tobacco to the pocket when she said quickly: "Go on and smoke. I like it."

She watched the sure play of his fingers as he rolled the cigarette, saying wonderingly as he gave the wheat straw paper its final lick: "Do you suppose Ralph can do it that well?"

He grinned. "He can if he's been long in this country." A thought made him eye her more directly. "Ralph? Who's he?"

"My brother. I'm meeting him in Summit. It's been four years since I saw him. And then it was only for a few weeks on one of his rare trips home."

Instantly a reserve settled across his face. She didn't notice because it passed so quickly. And Steve was thinking: *Couldn't be the same. But Ralph did have a sister.* He tried to make his tone casual as he drawled: "I knew a Ralph Bates back a couple of years. Down in the Cimarron country,"

She shook her head. "A different one. My brother's Ralph Kinney. I'm Nora Kinney."

He nodded. "My handle's Steve Lord." That infectious smile touched his lean face once more. "One of the chosen few that gets sworn at every time he's called by name."

This brought an answering smile from her. But, oddly, a grave expression touched her eyes the next moment and she confided: "Maybe I shouldn't be telling you, but I'm worried about Ralph."

"Some kind of trouble?" It cost him a real effort to make the question sound offhand. He thought he knew what was coming.

Yet it wasn't quite what he expected, for she answered: "I wish I knew. You see, I haven't heard directly from Ralph for some time. He doesn't know I'm coming."

He couldn't, Steve was telling himself as he drawled noncommittally: "He'll be glad to see you."

"I wonder." She sat in silence for so long a time that he decided she wasn't going to speak again. Then abruptly she was asking in a low voice, so as not to waken the others: "Do you know a man by the name of Foster in Summit? Edward Foster. He's Ralph's partner."

"This is my first time up here." He was giving her only a half truth, for he did know Ed Foster—or of the man. There was a week-old letter from Foster in his coat pocket.

"He wrote me at home about three weeks ago," Nora went on, "saying he thought it would do Ralph good to have me out here. He especially wanted me not to tell Ralph I was coming. He mentioned that they were building a new school in Summit and needed a teacher, in case it turned out I should want to stay on. Of course he knew that I had no family. Now doesn't that seem strange to you?"

"How?"

"His not wanting Ralph to know. It's almost as though Ralph wouldn't have wanted me to come. Why?"

Steve only shook his head, saying nothing yet thinking: She's in for a jolt. For some minutes he wondered how he could save her the grief he knew was in store for her. But in the end he saw no way. And when the sun presently edged over the peaks and slanted its strong glare in at the coach window, waking the man opposite, Steve was almost thankful that their privacy had been invaded and that Nora would now be reluctant to say anything further.

He thought about the letter in his pocket again. Foster hadn't said much, only just enough. His last sentence was the one that stuck in Steve's mind: *Knowing you were his best friend, I thought you might want to come up here and look into the matter.*

Yes, Steve wanted to look into it. For Ralph was dead.

II

This was his eighth stop today at the door of the shack with the window bearing the legend: *Foster And Kinney, Assayers.* Dusk was thickening along the steep grade of Summit's single street and the town, lively enough by day, was taking on an even lustier quality now with wagonload after wagonload of men coming down the cañon road from the mines and dumping their cargoes before the saloons and eating houses.

The assay office's window was dark and Steve, disheartened by the day-long wait, this time didn't even bother trying the door. He had earlier inquired after Foster in both stores flanking the office, but no one seemed to know where the assayer could be found. So now Steve stood close by the door, idly listening to the chant of a barker in front of the Crestview, two doors below. The barker's stand and the saloon's front were illumined by two coal-oil flares hanging from the posts of the walk awning and the crowd was thickest there of anywhere along the street, passers-by having to detour out beyond the tie rail to make their way. There was a constant flow of traffic in and out of the swing doors, and Steve, remembering that this was Miles Young's saloon, wondered if more gold wasn't taken out of it than out of most of the mines up the cañon.

This evening he had paid $2 for a poor meal at Young's log hotel, the Mile High, and for the privilege of using a bunk in its huge upstairs room between the hours of midnight and 8:00 tomorrow morning, he was paying another $3. So Miles Young could count still another gold mine within the town limits of Summit, one that wasn't marked by the tipple of a muck dump.

Steve was beginning to feel restless and out of sorts at this enforced waiting. It didn't seem right to be loafing here, doing nothing, not even having learned of the circumstances surrounding Ralph's death. He had decided against making any direct inquiries about Ralph, chiefly because of Nora Kinney. He was embarrassed now over having kept secret his identity there on the stage this morning. For some strange reason he had shied away from telling her what he knew of Ralph, deciding to leave that task to Foster. Later, when she had the whole story, he would go to her and apologize, try and explain his reticence. He could only hope that she would understand. Meantime, scanning the hotel book this noon when he signed it, he discovered that she had taken one of the few single rooms the building offered. He had had only a brief glimpse of her since the stage had left her at the Mile High this morning. Along toward the middle of the afternoon he had by chance seen her getting out of a buggy in front of the hotel. He had been too far away to get a look at whoever drove the rig.

Now, standing there by the assay office door, he built a smoke and lit it, wondering how to spend the evening. He decided finally to try the Crestview and had taken a stride toward it when a voice behind him softly called: "Steve Lord?"

He wheeled around. The office door now stood open half a foot. Nothing showed in its dark-slitted opening, yet the voice came again: "Go on around at the back and I'll let you in." Then the door closed quickly at the approach of a pair of men coming along the walk.

A strong excitement ran through Steve at this furtive introduction to Ed Foster—for this could certainly be no one but the assayer, Ralph's partner. He waited until the two passers-by had gone on, then turned idly up the uneven stretch of graveled walk. Warned by Foster's manner, he scanned the street in both directions and made sure no one was close enough to spot him before he stepped into a narrow passageway between two buildings several doors above the assay office. He used the same precaution before entering the littered alley behind the buildings. And shortly, as he walked in on the shack's rear door, it opened silently before him.

A strong wariness gripped him as he stepped in through the dark opening and his hand instinctively traveled to the gun at his thigh when the door closed to smother him in a pitch blackness.

The same voice that had spoken to him on the street gave a gentle laugh behind him now, saying: "A hell of a thing, this hide-and-seek game, but we're being careful." And suddenly a match flared alight and Steve wheeled halfway around to see a spare middle-aged man reaching for a lamp on a bench at the front wall of this small room.

"I'm Ed Foster." The man put the chimney on the lamp and then turned, holding out a hand. A broad smile patterned his thin and homely face.

Steve shook the hand, liking its firm grip and the undisguised warmth of welcome in Foster's brown eyes. "Thanks for writing me," Steve said awkwardly, and then went over to the chair

Foster pulled out from the bench and was offering him.

"We're being careful," the assayer said once more, nodding to the single window with the blanket hung over it. He thought of something then and went to the door, throwing its hefty bolt to lock it. "No one's going to find this strange. It's usual to lock up when I'm running a test. Part of this business is to keep what I do under the hat." He gave Steve a slow, appraising glance, nodding finally. "I could've spotted you in a crowd, Steve. What was it Ralph called you? . . . 'a light-haired ranny with a clear blue eye and a set of shoulders like a buffalo.' Something like that. Then Nora pointed you out to me today on the street."

"You were the one in the buggy with her?"

Foster nodded, his expression taking on a slow gravity. "We had been out to the cemetery. She took it better than I expected. There's a lot of iron in that girl."

Steve was glancing around the room, noticing the double bunk in one inside corner, the washstand alongside it. There were clay retorts and a small charcoal furnace on the bench opposite a pair of delicate scales. It was hard to imagine Ralph's having worked and lived here, for what Steve knew of his friend had to do with a bunkhouse, with horses and saddles, ropes and branding irons.

Foster, watching him and somehow reading his thoughts, said: "I've packed Ralph's things away. He usually worked over there under the window."

"So he made himself into an assayer," Steve drawled wonderingly.

"A damned good one. Too good. In fact, that's why he got into trouble."

Steve's glance settled on the man. "You didn't say much about that." He turned the chair around now and sat in it, arms folded across its back.

"No, I didn't. You can never tell who's going to read a letter going out of here." Foster frowned. "You haven't let anyone know why you're here, have you?"

Steve shook his head and Foster breathed: "Good. Nora only knows you as a man who helped her get up here. By the way"—his eyes lighted up and he smiled broadly—"you've managed to make an enemy of the one man you should have stayed on friendly terms with if you hope to accomplish anything."

"Young?"

Foster nodded. He leaned back against the workbench now, taking two cigars from a pocket of his vest and offering Steve one. As they lighted their smokes, he said: "It won't take long to tell it. Ralph was a careful worker, always had his eyes open to things. Sometimes he saw more than I did. Too much, as it turned out. It's a pity it had to do with Miles Young. Ralph wasted no love on the man. A long time ago I knew he was headed for trouble with him."

"How come?"

"One night at the Crestview Ralph saw Two Card Grant clean a prospector of every ounce in his poke. With crooked cards, of course."

"He'd know a forked deck," Steve said. "I've seen him trim a tinhorn at his own game. He even taught me a few things about marked cards."

Foster nodded soberly. "For some reason he always nursed a grudge against Miles Young after that. It galled him to see what Young was getting away with in this town. And you remember how stubborn he could be. About the only thing he could do directly was watch Young's mining deals, since we run all the assays on Young's properties. It looked like Ralph would sooner or later run onto something. I didn't want him to. But he was bullheaded and had a chip on his shoulder. That's why I wrote Nora, suggesting she come out. I had the crazy notion she might calm him down and take his mind off this thing."

"He ran onto something before she could get here?"

"He did," the assayer said quietly, taking a long draw on his cigar and staring at Steve through the blue fog of smoke. "He was running a test on a sample brought in from Young's Grand Champion when he discovered this thing. It was wire gold, just a few bits of it, that set him to wondering. They've never taken any wire gold out of the mines on the north slope, and Young's Grand Champion is off there. It had been only a fair producer up until then and Young was trying to sell it. The sale hinged on this assay. And the test ran so high Ralph couldn't believe it. So that night he went to see Young about it, telling him he'd either uncovered some mighty rich ore or that the sample had been salted."

"Salted?"

"Free gold added. The wire and knowing it couldn't have come from the Champion was what made Ralph suspicious. Well, Miles Young just laughed it off, saying maybe he'd hang onto the mine after all. But Ralph told Young he was going to see that Swanson heard about it. Then. . . ."

"Who's Swanson?"

"The man that bought the Grand Champion from Young after Ralph died." Foster's tone was utterly serious now. "Ralph was on his way up the cañon to see Swanson when he was killed."

"By the way," Steve drawled tonelessly, "you didn't mention how they got him."

"Buckshot."

Foster's one word jolted Steve who breathed a long, slow sigh as he said: "Go on."

"Ralph had gold on him when he was killed. He always carried it and his poke was empty when they found him next morning. So we'll never know why he was killed, whether to keep him from seeing Swanson or simply to rob him."

"We'll know," Steve intoned softly, flatly.

"I hope we will," Foster said. "Ralph was a good man. Too good to die this way."

"It could've been Young?"

Ed Foster shrugged his thin shoulders. "Could have been, yes. He made a chunk of money on the Grand Champion deal. Swanson's a comparatively poor man and right now he's barely meeting expenses. He blames Young, naturally, for misrepresenting things. But all Young does is refer to the test Ralph ran. Ralph naturally submitted a written report on it."

"Hasn't this Swanson come to you?"

"He has. And he hasn't learned a thing." A wry smile crossed Foster's face. "My friend, I'm in business here. Publicly I'm completely ignorant of how Ralph's test on the Grand Champion ran. If I ever hinted I knew something was wrong, I'd be where Ralph is."

"Don't you have a lawman here?"

Foster laughed. "Sure. A town marshal who used to be a bouncer for Young at the Crestview." He shook his head and with a guilty look went on. "I know what you're thinking. I should be doing something about this, one way or the other. I liked Ralph and a man sticks by his friends. But, Steve, I'm just one man against Young's pack of wolves. And I'm no hand with a gun. Young's got ten men, twenty if he wants, who would take his pay to kill any man he cared to point out. So I've kept this to myself because I want to stay alive."

His words quieted a small anger that had risen in Steve a few moments ago. Steve liked the assayer's forthrightness and honesty. And now he tilted his head in a nod, drawling: "In your place I'd do the same thing. But I won't hold off, Foster."

"I knew you wouldn't. That's why I wrote."

"Can you give me anything at all to go on?"

The assayer shook his head. "Not a thing except what Ralph told me."

"How about Swanson? Couldn't he help?"

"Not at all. He's simply been played for a sucker. Right now he's trying to get out from under, trying to sell the Grand Champion for exactly half what he put up for it."

Steve thought a moment. "I'll go see Young."

"You do and you're a dead man."

Steve's impulse was to protest Foster's ultimatum. But there was a finality about it that wouldn't bear arguing against. Miles Young ruled this town; there was no proof beyond Foster's suspicion of what lay behind Ralph's death. There was nothing to be done about it.

"That's all?" Steve asked.

"If there was more, I'd be giving it to you, Steve."

"How much of this does the girl know?"

"Most of it. But I have her promise she won't go to Young, won't let anybody know she suspects anything."

Steve came erect now, carefully returning the chair to its place by the bench. He nodded to the door. "I'll be going."

Foster went to the lamp, holding his hand above it and turning down the wick as he gave Steve a last glance. "I'm sorry as hell, Steve. Wish I could help."

"We'll see how it goes," Steve drawled tonelessly.

"By the way, in case you want to see me again, you'd better make it after dark. You'll find the door locked. A couple of quick taps, then two slow ones will let me know who it is."

Steve nodded, the room went dark, and shortly the door swung open. Stepping out into the alley, Steve had never felt so alone, or so completely gripped by baffled anger.

III

He was eating breakfast in the shabby hotel dining room the next morning when Nora came in out of the small lobby. She looked around the room, saw him, and at once started toward his table. And, as he stood up, he was feeling fine once more, better than at any time since reaching Summit.

It was her smile that did it, the gladness and the warmth of it surprising him and quickening the interest that had been in him yesterday on the stage.

She said: "Good morning, Steve." Then, as he stood there too surprised to speak because she had addressed him so familiarly, she took the chair he offered, saying: "Last night I got to thinking about your name. It seemed I'd heard it before. Then later I was going through some letters of Ralph's and ran across it. You can't be anyone but his friend, Steve Lord."

His lean face colored guiltily and, sitting down again, he said awkwardly: "I should've told you right off. But I knew what had happened and. . . ."

"And you didn't want to hurt me. Wasn't that it?"

He nodded gratefully. "Never was much of a hand at that kind of a job. I'm sorry as can be about Ralph."

"Of course you are," she said softly, the brightness of her eyes for a moment betraying her grief. But then her head tilted bravely, stubbornly, and she said: "I've decided to stay on a few days."

"Stay on? In this sorry layout? Why?"

"Because you're here. Last night before I read Ralph's letter, I was ready to take the morning stage out. Then when I was sure it couldn't be anyone but you, I decided to stay."

"But why, miss? I. . . ."

"You'd better start calling me Nora, Steve," she interrupted. Then she continued seriously: "You're here to do something about this, aren't you? About the way Ralph died?"

"That's why I came," he admitted. "But there's blessed little to go on."

A bright surface light of anger touched her eyes. "We know that Miles Young did it, don't we?"

"Not for sure."

She seemed shocked. "But how can you say that? Ed Foster believes Young killed Ralph. Or had him killed."

Steve grinned helplessly. "Take it easy. You've got the bit in your teeth. Ed's not sure of anything. Neither am I . . . yet."

A vast relief made her face striking-looking, almost radiant. "Good, Steve. Then you're going to do something about it, after all. Can you tell me what it is?"

He couldn't disappoint her, yet it took him a long moment to find an answer. "Thought I'd start by calling on this Swanson. The one that bought Young's mine."

"Can I go with you?"

He shook his head. "Not if we're to get very far. No one knows what I'm here for. Plenty of people must know you by now. It wouldn't help much if Miles Young found we were out to nail his hide."

"But we're together right now, Steve."

"Sure. We met on the stage. Young even saw us. He can't make any medicine of that."

She didn't like it much but said gracefully: "All right, we're simply chance acquaintances. But I'll have to see you now and then, Steve."

"Ed Foster can rig that."

A waiter with a dirty flour-sacking apron brought Steve his plate of food. Nora ordered her breakfast and over the next half hour Steve set about getting to know this girl whose brother had been so close to him.

It was raining that night when Steve turned into the head of the alley and made his way down it to the door of the assay office. A ribbon of light showed under the door and when he softly knocked—the two quick taps, then the two slower ones Foster had suggested—the slit of light blacked out and he heard a step come to the door. He stood with his wide shoulders hunched under the streaming poncho, head tilted so that the water dripped from the channel at the front of his wide hat.

The door opened suddenly, nothing showing in its black rectangle for a moment. Then Ed Foster's indistinct shape moved against the blackness and he said: "Come on in."

When the door was bolted and the lamp lighted again, Foster was smiling. He drawled: "You've got a way of getting around, friend. Tell me what it's all about."

Steve shed the poncho, tossing it to the floor by the door. "I went up there to see Swanson."

"So I hear. He was in tonight asking about you."

"What did you tell him?"

"I'd never heard of you before. And Randall was here, too. What's the play, Steve? Randall's asking half again as much as his mine's worth."

Steve smiled thinly. "I'm buying some property for an Eastern outfit, looking 'em all over."

Foster eyed him speculatively. "Go on. I still don't get it."

"You will in the end. Meantime, can you put me onto a man who'll sell me eight or ten ounces of gold and keep quiet about it?"

Foster nodded to a small square safe sitting under the near end of his workbench. "You're talking to that man."

Steve held out a hand. "Good. You'll have to trust me with it, Ed. I laid out my last dollar ten minutes ago buying a six month's option on the Grand Champion."

An alarmed look came to Foster's thin face. "At what price?"

"What he was asking, fifteen thousand."

"You'll lose your shirt, man," Foster breathed.

"Guess again, Ed," Steve drawled cryptically.

The assayer was silent a long moment, then said irritably: "Don't keep a man waiting. Tell me what the play is."

Steve told him, yet that worried expression clung to Foster's face and in the end, when Steve had finished, he shook his head and said: "Those are long odds you're playing. Too damned long."

"Not if you'll play along with me. Ed, Swanson took me down in that hole today. What's a closed-off stope?"

"A boarded-up tunnel. Why?"

"What did they find in the Grand Champion's closed-off stope? The south one, Swanson called it."

"Not a damned thing." Ed's look was puzzled now.

"Well, they're going to," Steve drawled. "That's where we'll make our start."

Ed shook his head, his look stubborn. "No. Swanson's got a good man bossing that crew, a hard-rock man."

"We'll fire him."

Now a slow smile crossed the assayer's features and he said quietly: "Come to think of it, we could keep that man and maybe use him. He lost a winter's pay at a poker layout there in the Crestview about a month ago. So he can't be wasting much love on Miles Young. His name's Boyle, Sam Boyle. He'd play along with us."

"You're not having anything to do with it," Steve told him. "I've thought it all out. I'm even going to have another assayer run the test. Is there another?"

"Jenkins, down at the far end of the street." Ed was disappointed and his look plainly showed it. "Why not let me do it?"

"We wouldn't want to run a chance of Young tying you into this, would we?"

"No," Ed admitted reluctantly. He gave Steve an odd glance,

drawling: "You're not thinking I'm yellow, are you?"

"Hell no."

The way Steve spoke let Ed know he was hearing the truth. He went to the safe now, his look one of relief, and, after he had twisted the combination and opened the door, he said: "Better let me hang onto this dust till you need it." He took out a sheaf of bills, handing them over to Steve. "But if you're working for a big Eastern operator, you'd better begin throwing money around. This'll start you. And if you say a damn' word about paying it back, I'll. . . ." He grinned, looking up at Steve. "Don't know what I would do. Anyway, half of what you've got there is Ralph's. He'd want to see it spent exactly as you're going to spend it."

Steve came in behind the customer at Two Card Grant's blackjack layout and tapped him on the shoulder. When the man looked around, Steve held out a $50 bill, drawling: "Like to trade places, neighbor?"

The man glanced at the money and a broad grin creased his bearded face. "I sure would, stranger," he said, and took the money. Two Card had observed all this with a gathering alarm betraying itself in his beady gray eyes. He stiffened now as Steve eased his long length into the chair opposite. He laid down the deck of cards he had been holding and glanced quickly behind him. The presence of a house man at the next layout seemed to bolster his nerve, for he smiled faintly and said: "Things were a sort of tight there the other night, eh?"

"Deal," Steve said flatly.

When Two Card nodded and started to pick up the cards, Steve drawled: "A fresh deck."

Two Card called the house man across, spoke to him briefly, and the house man went to the bar and came back with a new deck of cards. He handed them to Two Card and then took a stance to the gambler's left, behind his chair. And Steve understood that some signal had passed between them, that the house man had been warned to stay close. He didn't care.

"These suit you?" Two Card asked, breaking open the new deck. When Steve merely nodded, the gambler's supple hands commenced the shuffle.

Steve was looking at the cards, thinking: *If Ralph could only be here.* He had spent the last ten minutes watching the play at several of the Crestview's layouts, making sure of something. Now he was even more sure. The saloon used only two types of cards, two almost identical decks. One was a straight one, an honest deck. The other—and this one was in use wherever a house man ran a layout—closely resembled the first but was a marked one of such a standard variety that Steve marveled at the gullibility of the saloon's customers. He could remember a certain night when he and Ralph had strapped a tinhorn using a deck like this before running him out of town. Afterward, Ralph had taught him the markings on the cards and the two of them had run a sandy in the bunkhouse one payday night, cleaning every man of the crew before they let them in on the joke.

Now, as Two Card started the deal, Steve was watching the cards and slowly remembering what the markings meant. By the end of the first two hands it was coming back to him. Two Card took $10 of his money the first hand; they split the second. Before the next deal began, Steve asked: "What's your limit?"

Two Card looked at the beamed ceiling. "The sky."

Steve took out the roll of banknotes Ed Foster had given him, counting to see how much he had. It totaled $570. He separated $70 from the bundle and put it in his pocket. "Five hundred," he said, laying the rest in front of him.

"Without even a look at your down card?" the gambler queried, smiling thinly, confidently.

Steve eyed him impassively, drawling: "You talk too much."

Two Card sobered and dealt. Steve, with an eight down and a five showing, looked at the top card of the deck, the one he would get if he called for another. It was another eight. He saw that Two Card had a ten down. He said—"Hit me."—then—"Enough."—when he had the eight up and a total of twenty-one.

Two Card knew he was beaten even before he turned up a jack, yet tried to school his expression to one of polite inquiry before Steve turned up the winning card. "Not bad," Two Card said, and paid off,

Steve pocketed the $500 he had won and let his original bet ride. He won the next hand, purposely lost the following one. And now the word was getting around that a big game was under way and several men drifted across from the bar and surrounding layouts to look on. The house man, standing behind Two Card, shifted nervously, his hard glance clinging to Steve as the play was resumed.

It went on that way for another twenty minutes, Steve regulating his winnings so that nothing was obvious. Once he bet $1,000 and lost, and afterward pretended to be nervous and called for a drink. But then he won the next bet of $1,000, and the next.

By the time he was $5,000 the winner, there were men watching who had deserted several other nearby tables. Two Card seemed outwardly as impassive as ever, yet Steve noticed that a beady perspiration was showing on the gambler's upper lip even though the air in here was only comfortably warm.

It was going on that way, a see-saw game gradually adding to Steve's winnings, when Miles Young's high shape sauntered out of his office beyond the bar and joined the crowd around the layout.

The saloon owner towered a full head over any other man present. Steve looked up at him. Young nodded, smiling faintly.

Then Steve took out all his winnings, counted them, and laid them in one stack on the table. "Sixty-five hundred," he drawled.

Two Card hesitated. He was undecided and looked around, noticing for the first time that Young was watching. The saloon owner gave him a barely perceptible nod and Two Card shuffled the deck.

"Lay it on the table," Steve drawled.

"Lay what?" Two Card bridled.

"The deck," Steve answered quietly. And several of the onlookers softly laughed.

Two Card's face lost some of its paleness before a flush of anger as he put the cards on the green-felted table. Steve had already cut the deck but now noticed that the card he'd left on top was no longer showing. The gambler had somehow managed to palm it while handling the deck.

He reached brazenly across and picked up the cards, shuffling them, cutting them three times before a ten showed, then putting them back. He drawled pointedly: "Just let 'em lay and use the top ones."

Men within a radius of fifteen feet of the table heard him speak. It was quiet here at the front of the room now. Off to the left in the far corner nothing but empty chairs circled a poker layout, something that hadn't happened in the Crestview at this time of night since the day it opened its doors. The onlookers were tense. The house man behind Two Card was fiddling nervously with the front of his coat, running a thumb in and out of a buttonhole. Even Miles Young was showing the tension; he had lighted a cigar and now puffed at it so rapidly that it was drawing hot, biting his tongue.

Two Card gave Steve the ten and had to take a four beneath it. The next down card showing Steve knew to be a ten even before Two Card flicked it at him face up. He had a total of twenty, with anything over twenty-one retiring him if he drew another card.

He looked briefly at the deck, seeing the markings of an ace on the top card. He said idly: "Another."

Two Card's face blanched in anger as he turned up the ace. For a moment it looked as though he would call Steve for taking the chance he had. But in the end he decided against it and, his forehead damp and his hand shaking, gave himself a seven and a nine to add to his four.

"You win," Two Card said in a shaking voice. Then he added: "The house closes the game. If you'll step on back to the office, we'll pay you off."

"What's the matter with my money?" Steve asked tartly.

And behind him a man's tense laugh sounded loudly across the stillness.

Miles Young's massive shape abruptly pushed through the circle of onlookers. He came in alongside Two Card, saying: "Nothing, stranger." He touched Two Card on the shoulder, signaling that he should leave the chair. When the gambler rose, Young sat down. He took a wallet from his pocket, counted out $6,500, and handed it across to Steve, saying: "Name your game."

"The same," Steve answered,

Young called for a new deck. No one spoke now as the house man went to the bar and brought back an unopened pack of cards. At the back of the room five men left a poker layout and hurried to join the crowd circling the table where Steve and Young faced each other.

"Want the deal?" Young asked as he broke open the new deck.

Steve only shook his head, his impassive look not betraying the excitement in him. Miles Young's broad and ruddy face wore a confident look. That look weakened perceptibly when Steve placed the bundle of banknotes Young had just given him on his original stack.

"All of it?" Young asked tonelessly, and again the only answer he had was a nod from Steve.

When the cards were offered him, Steve cut an ace the first time. "Again," Young said in a brittle voice, his eyes on the deck telling Steve he knew the markings of the cards as well as his gambler did.

So Steve cut again. And, unbelievably, a second time an ace topped the deck. "Once more," Young drawled.

Steve shook his head, asking mildly: "Why should I? What're you afraid of?"

A man standing directly behind his chair muttered: "Maybe he can read 'em, stranger."

Young's glance whipped wickedly up to the man and for a moment it looked as though he was coming up out of his chair. But then a studied impassiveness settled across his face and he picked up the cards, taking them in one hand.

"Flat on the table," Steve drawled.

Young took that studied insult with a smile, sensing that the crowd was against him. He dealt Steve the ace down, dealt himself a nine down. Steve's first up card was a five. Looking at the deck he saw he would get a four if he drew again. He said: "I stand."

A flush mounted quickly to Young's face. He eyed Steve with a hard glance. "What's the matter? Afraid?"

"You're going to bust your hand," Steve answered quietly. "Go ahead."

Young turned up the four to go with his down nine. The next card was a ten. The saloon man and Steve both knew what it was before Young disgustedly flicked it up.

A gasp, hushed and excited, rippled through the crowd as the card showed. Then a hum of talk filled the room briefly, only to die as every man's glance focused on Miles Young.

He felt the crowd's eye upon him and anger corded the

muscles along his jaw. He took the wallet from his pocket once more. He thumbed through the banknotes remaining in it and abruptly tossed it aside, saying in a chill voice: "Go, open the safe, Two Card." Even he wasn't prepared to meet the emergency of having to pay off a $13,000 win.

"You can wait for that." Steve tapped the stack of notes lying beside his cards. "Twenty-six thousand is the bet on the next hand."

"There'll be no next hand," Miles Young said tonelessly. "The house is closing this layout."

The hush that settled over the room now made plainly audible the scrape of a man's boot somewhere at the back fringe of the crowd. Steve regarded Young coldly a long moment, then drawled mildly: "And they told me this was a wide-open town."

Young had regained some of his composure and now managed a halfway convincing smile as he shook his head. "A man hogs his luck only so far in this establishment, stranger. You've had enough." He looked up at Two Card and gave a nod and the gambler pushed out through the crowd and disappeared into the office beyond the end of the bar.

The crowd around the table thinned quickly now as men drifted back to the bar and the deserted gambling layouts. By the time Two Card was back again, the room was filled with its usual sounds, the click of chips, a strong run of talk, the clink of glasses.

Two Card said—"Thirteen thousand."—and tossed a fist-thick bundle of banknotes to the table in front of Steve.

Steve didn't bother counting his winnings. He pocketed the money and rose. "Try us another time," Young said affably as Steve turned and headed for the swing doors. Steve didn't answer.

He didn't hurry but he didn't waste any time in leaving the Crestview. Once on the walk he swung quickly upstreet. As soon as the shadows closed about him in front of a darkened store, he wheeled into the next between buildings passageway he came to. Now he walked faster, and, as he went the length of the narrow corridor, he kept looking behind him.

He was almost at the rear of the buildings when he saw a man's indistinct shape appear at the head of the passageway, hesitate there a brief moment, then come on toward him. And now his hand dropped to thigh and came up fisting his Colt. A strong excitement rose in him, blending with a sudden urge of wild recklessness. He was enjoying this as he wheeled quietly out of the alley end of the passageway and swung so that his back touched the slab rear wall of the building.

Just then he saw a rain barrel sitting within arm's reach of him. A rough board eave spout dropped from the building's roof along the wall and right-angled to an end directly over the barrel. It took him only an instant to make up his mind. He reached into his coat pocket, took out the money, and stuffed it into the throat of the spout, reaching in far enough to wedge the big bundle of banknotes up above the elbow.

He had barely flattened to the wall once more when the slur of a scraping boot sounded close by. The next instant the man who was following him stepped warily out of the passageway's end.

Steve lifted the gun and whipped it down in a glancing blow at the side of the man's head. At the last moment, as his knees buckled, the man fell heavily into him. Steve had a passing glimpse of his victim's face as he was stepping clear. It was the house man who had stood next to Two Card during the game.

Another barely audible sound laid its strident warning along Steve's nerves that moment and he was lunging away, letting the house man fall, when a gun's closely confined explosion blasted at him from deep in the passageway. A chip flew from one of the slabs close alongside his face, striking him on the left cheek as he rocked his Colt into line.

He threw two thought-quick shots into the narrow corridor, and then wheeled back behind the protection of the nearest building's corner. A choked scream echoed hollowly out of the passageway. A moment later he heard the pound of boots sounding down the broad alley above him. He turned and ran.

He had taken only three strides when another gun exploded deafeningly from the deep obscurity of a building's rear wall close to his right. The air whip of the bullet touched the back of his neck and, without breaking stride, he rocked the .45 around and shot at the rosy wink of gun flame that had stabbed out at him a split second ago. Now he dodged from side to side as he ran on up the alley. Behind him he heard someone shout lustily. On the heel of that voice came a pound of boots from close ahead.

They had this alley closed at both ends. He made for the black outline of a shed off to his left and threw himself belly-down in the deep obscurity of a trash pile mounded against the side of the shed.

Suddenly a man ran past the shed, then stopped in plain sight, bawling: "That way, Len! He ain't been through here!"

Steve lined his sights at the man. Then, reluctantly, he eased his finger off the trigger. He had never liked a shot at sitting game, least of all a man, and the fact that this man worked for Miles Young made no difference. So he lay there, checking his labored breathing, watching as the man roved the shadows behind a store, then came back to stand where he first had.

Shortly this man was joined by a second and for perhaps a quarter minute the two stood there, talking in low tones, their words unintelligible to Steve. Then finally someone far up the alley hailed them and they walked slowly away, their guns still in their hands.

Steve picked himself up, brushed off his coat and pants, and crossed the alley at a walk. He used a passageway farther along to reach the street, then sauntered up the crowded walk toward the hotel. If anyone had seen anything odd in the sound of the shots, no one on the walk showed it. Steve climbed the hotel steps, took a quick glance both ways along the walk, and, when he saw no one he recognized, went on in.

He was groping his way from the dark upstairs hallway in through the bunkroom door when a solid blow at the back of his head filled his vision with a white blaze of light. He felt himself falling and that was the last he knew.

IV

Two Card had had a hard night and didn't come down from his second-floor room over the saloon until 11:00 that morning. One of the aprons brought his breakfast across. But after the first few mouthfuls Two Card pushed his plate aside with a wry grimace of distaste. He drank his coffee and called for another cup. It was being brought to him when Miles Young stepped out of the office, saw him, and sauntered over to the table to take the chair opposite.

For several seconds Young eyed his gambler silently. Then he said in an acid way: "You're losin' your touch, Two Card."

"You didn't do so well with him yourself." The gambler knew what Young meant and this slighting remark made of his trade didn't much improve his sour frame of mind.

"He could read those cards," Young said thoughtfully. "Now why didn't we have the sense to see it and use a straight deck?"

"He couldn't read 'em," Two Card insisted. "It was plain luck. That and his making us keep the deck out of our hands. Think he'll be back?"

"After what we did to him later?" Young shook his head. "No, besides he's spent the money."

Two Card frowned worriedly. "Just what happened to it? Len

says he even went over the lining of his coat."

"Who cares?" Young shrugged his heavy shoulders. "The point is, all he's got is a sore head this morning while I'm having to bury a man and pay a sawbones to take lead out of another's shoulder. Now he's bought the Grand Champion from Swanson with my cash."

"He's what!" Two Card's head jerked up and he spilled some of the coffee from the cup he was lifting to his mouth.

"Bought the Grand Champion. And they say he's dickering with Randall to take over the Lolita."

Puzzlement showed strongly on Two Card's face. "What would a cow nurse know about mines?"

"Suppose he isn't what we take him for? He could be a mining engineer rigged out as a saddle tramp. According to Sam Boyle up at the Champion, he knows plenty about what goes on underground."

"How would you know what Sam Boyle thinks?" Two Card asked pointedly.

"I've had a man working for Boyle ever since I sold Swanson the outfit. Ray Chase."

"But why would a smart mining man want to buy that played-out hole?"

"Search me. But this morning this Steve Lord was right down that hole with the crew, helping them tear out the planking closing off that south stope on the second level."

"Why?"

"How the hell would I know why?" Young snapped, his patience at an end. "But he had a chart of the layout with him and a copy of that survey the Boston geologist drew up last winter. Then there's what Randall said about him."

"What?"

"That he represents some big outfit in the East."

Two Card considered this in thoughtful silence and presently

Young went on: "He's played us for suckers twice now, Two Card. Maybe he'll try it a third time."

"How could he?"

Young leaned forward, putting his elbows on the table and frowning as he said: "I wish I knew. But if he runs onto something up there at the Champion, I'll damn' soon know."

Steve's waist overalls were powdered with granite dust and the polish was gone from his boots as he stepped out of the cage hoist and followed the Grand Champion's eight-man crew down past the muck chute. His wide hat sat on the back of his blond head out of respect for a swelling over his right temple and the calluses on his big hands were tender from having swung a jack-hammer most of the afternoon. But he was feeling fine, better than in a long time.

He said—"See you tomorrow."—as he left the man walking alongside him, turning up the office path. The others continued on down to where an ore wagon stood, ready to take them on into Summit.

Sam Boyle waited in the office, a stubby briar pipe slanted out of his mustached, ruddy face. And as Steve closed the door, Boyle drawled: "Well?"

Steve nodded. "You were right about Ray Chase. Saw him filling his dinner bucket with rubble brought down by the last charge you blew in the south stope."

Excitement flared in the Irishman's eyes. "You'd sprinkled that dust around Foster gave you?"

"All of it."

Boyle rubbed his hands together, grinning broadly. "I'll lay you ten bucks to one Miles Young is beating on Ed Foster's door inside an hour, wanting him to run a test on that stuff Chase is bringing him."

"Would I bet against myself?"

"No, you wouldn't," Boyle said soberly. "So your hunch on Young having a man here paid off."

"We'll see."

"Couldn't be anyone but Chase. I know the others. They wouldn't pour water down Young's throat if his innards were afire." The mine foreman eyed Steve worriedly. "You sure you want to be on your own tonight?"

"They'll let me alone from now on. Young won't try any more strong-arm plays. If this works, he'll be around wanting to shake hands."

"He'd never get the chance to shake my hand," Boyle growled.

Steve went to the water bucket, drank a dipperful, and then filled the basin on the bench alongside. He was soaping his face as Boyle asked: "How come you're running your assay through Jenkins instead of Ed Foster tomorrow?"

"Want to keep Ed out of it." Steve sloshed water into his face, saying as he reached for the towel: "Chase heard me tell one of the boys I thought Ed had missed a bet on the assay that made Swanson close off that stope. That'll get back to Young if we're playing the right hunch on Chase."

"Sort of hard on Ed, isn't it? He gets all Young's business."

Steve looked around at the Irishman, asking in a dry way: "You think Ed'll mind anything we do to even the score for Ralph?"

"No, sorry I said that," Sam Boyle answered quietly. "Ralph was a good man."

Steve left the mine corral as dusk was settling along the cañon, thinking how fortunate he was in having found a man like Sam to work with. He had had to put his blind trust in the mine foreman this morning after completing the deal with Swanson. "Here's wishing you luck with it, Lord," Swanson had said as he handed over the signed papers. "I've had damned little." And now Steve wondered if he was asking too much of his luck.

This had been a long day. He had slept only fitfully last night, the throb of his aching head making him restless. Finally, along about 4:00 this morning, he had become impatient at trying to sleep and had left the hotel and retrieved his money from the eave spout there behind the store in the alley. Then he had taken a roundabout way through the sleeping town to Ed Foster's shack. He had wakened the assayer and Ed had given him the gold. He had been at the Grand Champion in time to eat breakfast with Boyle and Swanson, and they had settled the details of the mine's purchase before they got up from the table. Later, playing Ed's hunch on Sam Boyle, Steve had told the foreman what he intended doing. And Sam Boyle had been delighted at the prospect, genuinely so, wanting to help in any way he could so long as it hurt Young.

So Steve had played his hand and there was no telling how it would turn out. Meantime he had enjoyed this quarter hour in the saddle that ended now as he brought the lights of Summit into view below along the crooked road. He was thinking of Ralph, and of Nora, as he reached the upper edge of the town.

He made a point of not eating his supper at the hotel, not wanting to run the chance of meeting Nora or of being seen with her. He was finishing his solitary meal in a small eat shack below the hotel when Two Card came in off the street, walked the length of the counter, and stopped alongside his table. The gambler nodded politely. " 'Evening."

Steve sat staring up at him, not answering his greeting. And shortly Two Card went on: "The boss would like to see you."

"Bring him on in."

"He'd like to see you in his office."

Steve smiled sparely. "He can walk, can't he?"

Two Card's eyes sharpened with hostility. He was at a loss

for a moment. Then he gave a nod and turned from the table to head for the street again.

In a surprisingly short time Miles Young's high shape was coming in off the walk, his head hunched to keep from hitting it against the top of the door frame. The saloon man was alone and came straight on back to Steve's table, pulling out a chair, and then asking before he took it: "Mind if I sit?"

"Go ahead." Steve was rolling a smoke and now gave particular attention to the way he was doing it.

"Hear a couple of my men got out of hand last night," Young said as he took the chair.

"So they worked for you?"

Young nodded, smiling a little now. "Guess the sight of you packin' all that money away got the best of 'em. You've got my apology, Lord."

Steve shrugged. "No harm done. Mixing it a little now and then never hurts a man."

"It hurt Ben Ames. We buried him this morning."

"Now did you?" Steve asked blandly. He wasn't surprised.

The saloon owner lifted his heavy shoulders in a gesture eloquent of his unconcern. "Ben wasn't worth much."

Steve said nothing, waiting for Young to show his hand. The way the man did it was anything but casual as he now said: "They tell me you've bought yourself a mine with your last night's winnin's."

"That's right."

"Or was it your money?"

Steve decided to offer Young the bait and nodded: "My money this time. It's a good feeling. Usually I'm handling someone else's."

"You work for somebody?"

"Peabody and Flint of New York." These were the first names that occurred to Steve.

"Big outfit?"

"Not too big for back there," Steve drawled. "Ten million might buy them out."

Young was impressed and couldn't quite school his expression to hide it. "So this Grand Champion deal is your own," he mused, abruptly asking: "How does it look?"

"I'll know in a couple of days."

"Then what?"

"Who can tell? I may hang onto it or take a profit and get out from under. A mine's always a risky bet except for the long pull. But I can't keep my stake tied up forever." Steve's tone was matter-of-fact, almost bored.

Young eyed him a moment with an unfeigned respect before he let his face settle back to its impassiveness. Then he was saying: "You're a gambler, so am I. How about selling the Champion at a profit right now? Tonight."

There was no pretense backing Steve's look of surprise. He had been expecting some such thing as this but hadn't looked for it to come so soon or so bluntly. All he could think of to say now was: "Why should I?"

"I called you a gambler. You wouldn't have bought the Champion unless you were one. You're an engineer and you know your business. So I'd be gambling on that, on the Champion being worth more than you paid for it. If you sold to me, you'd be making a nice piece of change without lifting a finger."

Steve appeared to give the matter some deliberate thought. "What's your idea of a nice piece of change?"

"Twenty thousand. A profit of five thousand in a single day." Young eased back in his chair, brushing his coat aside and hanging his thumbs from the armholes of his vest, smugly asking: "How does it sound?"

Steve laughed. "Do you reckon I'd put fifteen thousand in a

thing expecting to get back only twenty? Uhn-uh."

"I could go as high as twenty-five," Young insisted smoothly.

"You'd have to double that before I'd listen."

Now Young straightened in his chair once more, his look becoming more alert: "Suppose I did double it?"

"Why the hell would you with nothing to go on?"

"Because I play hunches."

Steve sobered, asking tonelessly: "You mean you're offering fifty thousand for the Champion?"

"I am. Here and now." Young's hand dipped inside his coat and came out with the wallet Steve had seen before. It bulged a good bit fatter than it had last night, and, when the saloon man drew a packet of banknotes from it, Steve saw that each was a $1,000 bill.

"That's my offer. No strings attached. No guarantees, nothing." Miles Young began thumbing through the bills, counting them. Steve sat watching, trying to keep a straight face.

It took Young a good quarter minute to count the money. Finished, he pocketed the considerably thinned wallet, picked up the banknotes with one hand, and slapped them across his other opened palm. "Fifty thousand, Lord. Federal banknotes. And not a damned thing asked in exchange except the deed to the Champion with your signature."

Steve appeared to hesitate. He said haltingly: "There'll be no hold-up there. I've got the deed with me."

"Then get it out." Young was hardly able to control his eagerness,

Reluctantly almost, Steve took the deed to the Champion from his pocket. Young turned to call to the man behind the counter: "How about a pen and some ink, George?"

The waiter nodded and brought a bottle of ink and a pen across and set them on the table, his eyes bugging at sight of the money. Then Steve deliberately dipped the pen and signed over the deed, saying as he finally offered it: "Hope you know what you're doing. I don't."

"I do," Young drawled.

A broad smile broke across his face. He pocketed the deed and pushed the money across to Steve. "You damned fool," he said softly. "That rock you blew out of the end of that stope today will run a thousand to the ton."

Steve wasn't looking for what happened next. Young's right hand slid smoothly into sight. The saloon owner laid the barrel of a .45 on the edge or the table, saying flatly: "Just in case you decide to change your mind, my friend. This time I'm the winner. Half a million couldn't buy you back the Champion."

He rose cautiously and pushed back his chair. That gloating, satisfied smile didn't break from his face as he backed to the door and out through it.

The man behind the counter had watched all this, and now, his alarmed glance coming back to Steve, he asked: "What was ailin' Young?"

A slow smile patterned Steve's face. "Plenty. But he doesn't know it just yet."

V

Nothing in Steve's experience was quite like the feeling he carried away with him from the restaurant. He felt let-down and weary. Even the awkward bulge of his coat—where the sheaf of banknotes stuffed the inside pocket—failed to lift his spirits. He was reminded that he should probably be watchful now as he headed up the walk, for $50,000 was considerable money and last night's violence over a lesser amount was still fresh in his mind. But all he thought was: *The hell with it!* He had never cared much about money—enough to get by on was all a man needed—and he had never understood the worship of it. So now he took no satisfaction at all in having deceived Miles Young.

There'll be more to it was the only thought that consoled him. This sale of the Grand Champion to Young was but a prelude of things to come, of things he hoped would even the score for Ralph.

But the more he thought of what was to come next the more uncertain he became. Suppose Miles Young didn't react in the way he counted on? Suppose the Grand Champion, through some quirk of fate, did pay off as the saloon man had been deceived into thinking it would? Then what Steve had done would be made pointless, and Young, if he had really killed Ralph, would go unpunished.

Now Steve was almost sure he had made a mistake, a costly one. Sooner or later Young would be warned of him and take the necessary precautions for protecting himself. Why hadn't he gone straight to the man that first day and accused him, shot it out with him without going to the pains of trying this elaborate revenge? But there were annoying answers to that, too—the lack of proof against Young, plus the risk of exposing Ed Foster. Steve was strictly alone in this and had been from the beginning.

With his thoughts fast becoming a meaningless jumble of uncertainties, he wondered for the first time about the money, about what to do with it. Strangely enough he hadn't yet given this a thought, although for the last day he had planned more or less for the eventuality of Young's turning over some sizeable sum. He would, of course, make up Swanson's loss on the Grand Champion, for that loss had been taken because Ralph had never reached the man to tell him of his suspicions, to warn him not to buy the mine. Ed Foster could probably use a chunk of the money. Nora would get the largest share. She had come out here counting on Ralph, and Steve, knowing she had no family, judged that this prospect of being on her own must have caught her unprepared and very probably in poor circumstances.

Now as Steve thought of Nora, he found himself suddenly hungry for the sight of her. Or was it merely that he wanted her assurances that he had done his best with Young? This thought halted him in his aimless stroll along the crowded walk. He had turned about and taken several strides back toward the hotel when he stopped abruptly before a remote suspicion that only self-pity backed his urge to go to her. He was intolerant of that and at once knew that he wouldn't see her.

So he turned across the street and went into a saloon, its din and stale air striking him as forcibly as a blow, at once taking his mind away from himself. He picked a spot far down along the bar and called for whiskey. Yet when the liquor burned his throat, he found no satisfaction in the taste of it and let the glass sit at his elbow only half empty.

Idly he began listening to the talk of a man nearby that rose over the tinny beat of a piano sounding from the small dance floor at the rear of the barn-like room. The man was saying: ". . . got it for a song, only fifty thousand. Damned if he didn't hire a dozen men right there at his bar, load 'em into a wagon, and haul em up there to start work tonight. He's rich, wallowin' in money now. Said he'd hire every pick and shovel man he could lay hands on at ten a day. I'm signin' on with the Champion tomorrow, brother."

Here was news that brought a thin smile to Steve's face. Young's greed wasn't letting him wait even overnight to cash in on his find. How long would it take him to discover how wrong he'd been about the Champion?

Steve loafed there at the bar for better than an hour, forcing himself to finish that first drink, and then down another. And gradually the bleak run of his thoughts eased off until finally he knew he would have to see Ed Foster tonight and talk with him.

Between them they might be able to figure out what was to happen next.

Tonight he was very careful in his approach to the assay shack, going almost as far as the upper edge of town before cutting over to the alley. But his knock on the shack's rear door went unanswered. No light showed beneath the door, and, as he idled there in the darkness, scanning the farther shadows, a vague uneasiness stirred in him. Ed should be here, waiting for word from him, especially after having run that test for Young on the sample Chase had stolen from the reopened stope.

In the end, he couldn't think of anything to do but wait. So he went on up the alley until he came to a stack of cordwood piled along the rear wall of a store. He leaned there and rolled a smoke. He hunched down behind the wood as he lit his match, cupping its flame in his bands to hide the light, and afterward he took care in shielding the cigarette's glowing end.

The minutes ran on with muffled sounds echoing in off the street to tell him that Summit was enjoying another of its lusty, bawdy nights. Once a man far gone with liquor stumbled up the alley and staggered past, singing discordantly and happily, and Steve almost envied him his stupor, his obvious ease of mind.

Shortly after the drunk had walked out of sight another shape moved into his sight out of the deep shadows along the rear of the stores. In several seconds he realized it was a woman. And when she stopped, then walked in on Ed Foster's door, he was at once curious.

He heard her knock and then wait out a long interval. Then she rapped on the door again, softly calling: "Ed."

He recognized Nora's voice at once and walked down to her, seeing the startled way she turned at the sound of his steps. "It's all right, Nora," he said quickly.

Standing close to her, the starlight let him make out the glad smile she had for him. "Steve," she breathed excitedly, "it's all over town. You did it."

He shook his head. "Nothing that'll even things for Ralph."

"No," she admitted, "but this will hurt him. You've done enough. Ed said this afternoon you should leave even if you didn't manage what you have."

It was on the tip of his tongue to protest that. But then he saw how foolish it was to worry her and drawled: "That's an idea."

"You must leave, Steve," she insisted. "Ed says it's even dangerous for me to be seen coming here. Think what it must be for you. Think what would happen if you were around when Young finds out what you've done to him."

"Won't like it much, will he?" A disarming grin crossed his face. "But how about you?"

It was several seconds before she answered lifelessly: "I'm here, Steve. One place is as good as the next now. Ed says they'll give me that job of teaching in the school. And," she added quietly, "Ralph's here."

"But so's Miles Young. You'd spend your time hating him, wishing something would happen to him. That's no future for you."

"It's the one I want, Steve. I'll be on his conscience." There was a strong edge of pride in her voice. "Every time he sees me, he'll remember Ralph and what he did. Then maybe someday there will be enough decent people here to drive him out. I want to be here when that happens. I'll want him to know I had a hand in it."

"But that may take. . . ."

A sound from inside made Steve halt in mid-sentence. He saw a sliver of light suddenly shine from beneath the door. He listened a moment to the sound of movement in there and was finally sure it was just one man. Then he knocked softly and waited.

Tonight Ed Foster opened the door without bothering to turn out the lamp. He seemed unsurprised at seeing who it was and said: "Come on in. No chance of your being seen. Young and his whole crew are up at the mine. Steve," he added excitedly, "he dragged me up there while he put a crew to work dynamiting deeper into that stope. Made me run an assay right there in Boyle's shop. Give a guess on what the test showed."

When Steve shook his head, Ed closed the door and faced around again with a broad smile. "Just a trace of color, not enough to make it worth their bother hauling it down to the smelter. Which is what Ralph's assay showed." He nodded to his workbench. "I lied, told him Boyle's equipment was too crude to work with. So he's given me until morning to run the test here."

"Then get at it. We'll watch."

"But there's no point in doing it. I saw enough up there. And I wanted to see you before I broke the news to him." Now Ed glanced at Nora, saying gravely: "I had some fool notion of signing Ralph's name to the report. Just to smack Young between the eyes with what we've done to him."

"You couldn't, Ed," the girl said in alarm. "He'd . . . why, there's no telling what he'd do to you. Wouldn't he know then what you suspect?"

Ed shrugged, letting out a long sigh. "Sure." He gave Steve a faintly smiling glance. "But I'm tired of looking out for myself. I'd hold my head a damn' sight higher if I got in my lick at Young. So far I've been left out of it."

"On purpose, fella. You aren't. . . ."

"But I want to be in on it," Ed flared, with a surprising anger, cutting Steve short. "Ralph worked his guts out here for over a year with me, making this thing go. I owe him a lot. Now you want me to sit back and let someone else even the score for him." His look became apologetic as he added with his usual mildness: "I know it's asking for trouble, Steve, but I want it that way."

Regarding the assayer, Steve saw how much in deadly earnest he was. And he quickly decided to let the man keep his pride, drawling: "OK, Ed. Go ahead with it."

The gratefulness that showed in Ed Foster's eyes was touching. He said—"Thanks, both of you."—and stepped over to the bench to take a tablet from a shelf above it. This was a tablet of printed assay forms, and, as he uncorked a bottle of ink and reached for a pen, he drawled: "We'll make it even worse than it is, seven dollars to the ton." And as he started writing, Steve and Nora moved over to him and stood watching.

The form filled out, he hesitated over the line marked *signature* at the bottom of the sheet. Then with a sure hand he scrawled boldly: *Ralph C. Kinney.*

He was laying the pen aside when the street door's knob rattled and the panel swung abruptly open. Miles Young's bulky shape stood framed in the opening.

A shock of surprise at seeing who was here held the saloon man motionless a long moment. He was breathing heavily as though he had been walking fast. His glance ran quickly over each of them, finally settling on Steve who was watching the man's hands for some move that would signal an outbreak of violence.

But Young had so obviously not expected what confronted him now that Steve's wariness gradually eased away. Then the saloon owner was stepping into the room, asking: "Got a minute to spare, Foster?"

"Sure. What'll it be?"

Young closed the door and gave Ed a worried, half-angry look. "There's a joker hired on up there tonight that claims he knows how to run a test. Said he could do it in an hour. So I turned him loose on that layout in Boyle's office. Know what he claims?"

"No idea," Ed said quietly.

"Eleven to the ton! And he was workin' with the stuff we shot out of that new tunnel tonight."

Steve was about to say something but decided against it. This was Ed Foster's moment, and, watching the assayer, Steve was strangely proud of him. For now Ed stepped to the bench and without a word picked up his report and handed it to Young.

"I told him he was crazy," Young went on impatiently as he glanced down at the sheet of paper. His tone seemed relieved as he added: "Knew you'd get right busy on it when you got back here. Now what's this . . . ?"

The ruddiness was blanching from his face as he broke off his glance, whipping up to Ed: "What's this about seven dollars?"

Ed nodded. "To the ton."

Miles Young's eyes came wide open, shuttling across to Steve. "But that sample ran a thousand." His voice thundered in the confinement of this small room.

Again Ed Foster nodded. "It did, Young. Have you read the bottom line?"

Young glanced briefly at the sheet. And now the color rushed back into his face as rage tore through him. Then a cold calculating look was in his eyes as he looked at Nora. "Kinney? He's dead," he said tonelessly.

"He is," Steve drawled, "but if he's up there somewhere watching this, we knew he'd want to remind you."

"Of what?" Young slowly queried, a strong wariness in his glance now.

"Of the load of buckshot you planted in his back."

Miles Young read the finality in those words and for a moment they seemed to shock him. Then he did a strange thing.

He slowly smiled. It became a broad open smile, too, not just the beginning of one. And now Steve's glance left the man's face and shuttled to his hands once more as he was indefinably warned of some nameless danger.

Then Young drawled—"Take a look behind you."—speaking to Steve, no one else.

"You take it," Steve answered, not letting his glance stray.

"Two Card, you can have him," Young said.

Steve stiffened, chaining the impulse that wanted to send his hand to the gun at his thigh. The next instant a whisper of sound came from behind him and he was aware of Nora turning and of her quick intake of breath.

Steve sensed then that Two Card really was behind him, that the gambler had somehow managed to open the office's alley door without being heard. And only now did Steve realize the full extent of Miles Young's cunning, knowing Young probably never went anywhere, day or night, without being prepared for just such a circumstance as this.

He was careful not to move as Young came in alongside him and lifted the .45 from his holster. Only when the door closed behind him did he turn.

Two Card stood there with the Derringer Steve remembered so well fisted in a rock-steady hand. It wasn't much of a weapon. But at this distance it could break a man's back or tear a hole all the way to his heart.

"So you're all three in on it," Young drawled now.

"Not the girl," Steve quickly told him. "She just happened to be here."

"Just happened?" Young grinned wickedly. He looked at Ed. "Seven dollars to the ton is right?"

"Might be a trifle high," Ed said brazenly.

Young's glance came back to Steve. Suddenly he stepped in and pulled Steve's coat open, reaching into his pocket and taking out the money. "Then all we've had is an evening's entertainment," he said,

"Which isn't finished yet," Two Card reminded him.

"So it isn't."

There was a finality to Miles Young's words that drew Steve's nerves taut, that made Nora slowly move as far as she could from him, until her back was to the office's side wall.

Then Ed was saying brittlely: "Steve's right. Nora wasn't in on this."

"But she is now, isn't she?"

"No. She only knows what we've said. Nothing for sure."

Young looked at Nora. "Your brother was in my way," he stated flatly. "He'd been meddling in something he should have had the good sense to stay out of. That night he claimed he was going to Swanson with his report." His heavy shoulders lifted slowly, fell again. "So Two Card took care of him. With that iron he's got in his hand now. And it's loaded with buckshot the same as it was that night." The saloon man looked at Ed again. "Now she knows, doesn't she?" There was no mistaking his meaning.

Steve was watching Two Card. The man's shifty eyes were shuttling warily between the three of them and Steve was wondering if Ed could take advantage of the chance if he moved in on Two Card. But then the thought of what might happen to Nora paralyzed him, even though she stood well out of the way.

Nora spoke unexpectedly now, saying to Two Card: "All he has to do is tell you to kill and you simply do it?"

Humor touched Two Card's glance. "That's about it, miss."

"So he's made a murderer of you," the girl breathed, her look blazing hate at the gambler. "How does it feel?"

Two Card shrugged. "At first it bothered me, but that was a long time ago," he said with surprising frankness.

Just then Steve became aware of how surely she had caught

both men's attention, Two Card's and Young's. Miles Young stood there with Steve's gun hanging at his side, his faintly amused glance fully on the girl. And Two Card was watching her just as intently. And suddenly Steve understood that she was doing this with a purpose.

She went on in a tone of loathing: "You're almost proud of it, aren't you? Of your killing and your. . . ."

At that instant Steve lunged, taking the two strides between him and Miles Young. At the last moment, as Two Card's Derringer swung quickly around, a panic hit him. He clamped a hold on Young's lifting gun hand, pulled the man hard off balance, and wheeled fast behind him as he staggered.

The Derringer's explosion laid a deafening concussion across the room. A flood of pain stabbed the length of Steve's forearm and a numbness struck his hand so that Young's arm in its powerful upswing tore easily from his grasp.

Young choked off an outcry. His stagger became an ungainly lurch. In one lightning-swift moment Steve's .45 had thudded to the floor and Steve was realizing that Two Card, in trying for him as he dodged behind the massive man, had shot Young instead. Miles Young had staggered into the way of his own killer's gun.

Steve went to his knees, still shielded by Young as he fell. With his left hand he snatched up the Colt, drew back the hammer. And suddenly, as Young collapsed to the floor, Steve was staring across at Two Card and down the bore of the Derringer.

He dived sideways, whipping the Colt into line as he tried for the shelter of Young's outstretched bulk. He knew he was too late and tensed against the expected impact of the buckshot charge as he thumbed back the hammer of the .45.

At the last instant Two Card's eyes shifted momentarily from him and the gambler's weapon wavered. It was rocking back into line when Steve shot.

Two Card's checked vest stirred with the impact of the bullet. A look of incredulity crossed his face. He was slowly doubling over when another gun laid its deafening explosion across the room, sounding from Steve's right. The gambler was pounded erect again and his Derringer, dropping now, blasted on the heel of that other shot, the buckshot charge channeling a rough trough along the floor. Two Card fell with his face in that line of splinters.

Things went suddenly hazy for Steve. Pain throbbed along his right arm and he looked wonderingly to see his coat sleeve ripped about his forearm and his hand stained a bright crimson. He pushed up onto an elbow to see Ed standing alongside an open drawer of his workbench.

Ed held a smoking gun in his hand. Now he smiled wryly, drawling: "You could have given me that shot, Steve." But then a look of alarm crossed Ed's face and he quickly laid his gun down and came across to Steve.

Faintness hit Steve, and, when Ed had lifted him erect, he stayed on his feet only because Ed's arm was around him. As from a great distance he heard Ed say: "Help me get him to the bunk, Nora."

He felt the touch of Nora's hands on his good arm, felt her move his hand around her slender waist. He caught the fragrance of her hair as they helped him across to Ed's bunk.

"Let go, Steve," he heard Nora say finally. And the faintness left him and he realized he was standing there with his arm still around her, wanting to tell her something. *It can wait,* he told himself as he let them ease him down onto the bunk.

The pain came strongly then and for a time it dulled his senses so that he was only half aware of what went on in the room. Several other people were there, talking to Ed while Nora was working on his arm, bathing it, and then letting a bearded man in a black coat bandage it. The pain eased off and he heard the doctor telling Nora: "Those torn muscles take some mending. But with good care he'll never know it happened."

"He'll have good care," he heard Nora say.

Abruptly he was annoyed at lying here this way. He swung his boots from the bunk and sat up, supporting himself with his good arm. He saw that his other was bandaged and in a sling. The room was empty now and abruptly he realized that an uncertain span of time had passed without his being aware of it. As he looked out across the room, the doctor was just going out the door, Ed closing it after him.

When Ed saw him sitting there, he looked worried at first. Then he smiled relievedly: "Look at the patient, Nora."

"I've been looking at him." Nora's slender shape moved around from beyond the head of the bunk.

Looking up at her Steve thought he had never before seen a vision of such loveliness. His thought must have been mirrored in his eyes, for a look of gladness came to her face and her color heightened. "How is it?" she asked gently, a depth of emotion behind her words that was for him alone.

"A fool thing to do, keel over like that," he drawled.

"What's foolish about it? You're lucky you've got an arm left," Ed said. Then his seriousness vanished before a wide grin. "You've got the town stirred up, Steve. The hunt's on for Young's hardcases. A gang's headed for the Crestview to tear the place apart. Your fifty thousand is right here in my safe and. . . ." He paused, glancing at Nora. Her look made him softly laugh. "And you've got a nurse to see you on your feet again."

Ed did a strange thing then, turning to take his hat down from a peg on the door and saying gruffly: "Why should I tell you what you've got. I'll get out so you can enjoy it."

When the door closed behind him, Steve looked up at Nora. Abruptly he stood up off the bunk.

There was nothing to be said, for their eyes spoke their thoughts eloquently. She came close to him and his good arm went about her waist, drawing her to him.

★ ★ ★ ★ ★

Willow Basin

★ ★ ★ ★ ★

The author's original title for this story was "Willow Basin". Street & Smith's *Western Story* had previously serialized the first five Peter Dawson novels when the magazine was a weekly. Upon publication in the issue dated January, 1947, the title of this story was changed to "Willow Basin Outcast". The author's original title has now been restored.

I

This was the month of the winds and Pine City lay smothered in a haze of dust as Jim Roday looked down upon it for the first time in three years. Long streamers of grit lashed at the corner of the Western House from the sand flat along the creek, and the fine adobe dirt of the street was blown by the gusts. The walks were empty and the few buildings with shutters were using them. A wagon team at the hardware store rack stood awry and down-headed, hindquarters to the blast.

Jim Roday was restless and impatient after his long week in the saddle. He had expected to wait here until dark. But now the querulous voice of the wind seemed to be urging him on, telling him that this was no time to hesitate.

Finally it had its way, sending him up through the trees to the wash where he had tied his sorrel. He loosened the cinch and tested the knot in the reins and then walked back down the rocky slope, a tall man with a generous span of shoulders, outfitted in worn waist overalls, denim jumper, boots, and a wide hat. As he cleared the trees, his blue-eyed glance was fixed on one spot along the dust-fogged street below.

To reach the building on which his attention was fixed—a narrow deep adobe on the street's near side—he had to cross two hundred yards of open cedar-dotted ground, circle the livery corral, and take the alleyway alongside the barn. Reaching the plank walk, he paused a moment to glance casually first up and then down the street. No one was in sight, and, as he turned onto the walk, he drew his bandanna up over his nose and mouth. Swinging into the door of the scarred adobe, he thought: *Now if he's only in.*

He lifted a boot and kicked the door back and stepped through the opening, lazily lifting his Colt .45 out of its holster. Then he dropped the weapon back in its place, for the room was empty.

He drew a long sigh, disappointed, and let his glance run over the small cubicle. A roll-top desk with a brass lamp in one corner stood along the wall to his left. A caboose chair sat before the desk; two others, straight-backed and rickety, were along the front wall to either side of the window. At the back wall, a small safe was near the big nail-studded door that Jim knew led to the jail.

A litter of papers half covered the desk top along with others stuffed in the pigeonholes. These took Jim's attention and he went over there and rummaged through them. Not finding what he wanted, he opened the top drawer. A quick glance disappointed him. He shut the drawer and opened the next.

At the limit of his vision he was aware of a shadow passing the window. He straightened and turned as a blond man's thin shape blocked the doorway. He said explosively—"I'll be. . . ."—then lunged back as the man at the door swept his right hand up along thigh, drawing.

The shot blasted above the whine of the wind as Jim instinctively began his draw. The bullet tore through the bulge of his jumper as he quickly swung out of line and into the corner beyond the window.

"Bob, don't! Dammit, it's me, Jim!" His voice was muffled and he pulled the bandanna down.

There was a moment's silence before the man out there spoke. "Say that again."

"It's me. Jim Roday."

Riding in over the steady voice of the wind came a shout from somewhere across the street. Out on the walk, the man there answered loudly: "All a mistake, boys."

Then his spare frame wheeled in through the door. He slammed it shut, scowled as the broken latch didn't catch, and moved a chair over to prop it shut. Then, turning slowly, he faced Jim Roday, his weapon hanging at his side. A nickeled star was pinned to a pocket of his open vest.

"I'll be damned if it isn't," he breathed as he soberly surveyed his visitor and sheathed his gun.

But then alarm showed on his aquiline face and he said hurriedly: "Pull that blind." Stepping over to the desk, he wiped a match alight along the seat of his Levi's. As Jim Roday drew the torn blind down across the window, he lit the lamp.

Now a slow grin came to Jim's dark face as they looked at each other. He thumbed the Stetson to the back of his head. "Sheriff Rand," he queried. "Since when, Bob?"

"You loco fool," Bob Rand said sharply. You're crowding your luck, coming in here like this."

"You're doing the crowding. Came close to winging me."

"All I could see was someone going through my desk. Why'd you have your face covered?"

"I was primed to walk in on Ben Malley," Jim told him. "Wanted to surprise the old gent." His blue eyes looked pointedly at Rand's vest. "Since when the star?"

Rand seemed more at ease now. He took the chair at the desk as he said: "Ben's crippled. Rheumatism. They wished me off onto him as deputy last summer, then voted me in when he wouldn't run again." He frowned as he thought of something. "Shucks, I told you all this in letter."

"What letter?"

"The one I sent you in Silver City last January. Your father gave me the address."

"I move around," Jim drawled. "On purpose."

Rand's glance studied him carefully. "But you must've heard."

"Yeah," Jim said bleakly. "I've heard that a dodger's out on me. Heard it the hard way. From someone who tried to collect the reward."

Rand tilted back in his chair, took a sack of tobacco from vest pocket, and sifted a portion of the weed onto a wheat-straw paper. He offered the sack to Jim, who refused it. "So you know all about it?" he said.

"Just that I'm wanted for murder. This bounty hunter couldn't remember who I'm supposed to've killed. That's why I was going through the desk."

"You're telling the truth, aren't you?" Bob Rand said with awe. "You damned well don't know."

Jim didn't answer, waiting. Rand thumbed a match alight, lit his smoke.

"Hugh Hallett was killed last October," he told Jim. "Someone used a shotgun through a window of his cabin one night. While he was alone on the place. Mary and Bill were up in the hills with the roundup crew."

Shock ran through Jim, subsiding slowly. The pattern of his thinking was changing and it was several moments before he could rearrange it. "So they tied in that old rustling charge Hallett had against me and made their guess?" he said finally.

The sheriff nodded. "I did all I could for you, Jim. Even held back the story of the tracks until the inquest. But they put me under oath. Maybe because I was your friend."

"What tracks?"

"Up on the ridge east of Hallett's place. Ben sent me out to look around and I ran onto 'em. That bay stallion you rode out of here was the only animal there's ever been on this range with a shoe that big."

Jim stared at him levelly. "The bay pulled a tendon my first week out of here. I sold him for thirty dollars, to a nester near Big Springs. Three years ago."

Bob Rand lifted his hands in a helpless way. "Sure. I believe you. But no one knew about it."

Jim thrust his hands deep in pockets and stared down at the floor. "Go on," he said tonelessly. "Let's have the rest."

"The rest isn't much," Rand told him. "Mark Davies dug up what he could on that old charge and sold the jury on indicting you for murder. He even put up the reward."

Jim smiled meagerly. "So Davies still casts the big shadow around here?"

Rand nodded. "Bigger than ever. The best break I ever had was getting this job and leaving that outfit. This pays me less but I sleep a damned sight better."

"Who rods for him now?"

"Jeff Mears."

Thinking it out, Jim leaned down and beat the dust from his denims.

"So you play to lose any way you look at it," said Rand. "You'd better ride, friend. And ride far."

Jim ignored that. "How about Mary and Bill Hallett?" he asked.

"They're all right. Mary's grown up. Pretty. Bill still throws the money around like he had it."

"There was some paper on the outfit, wasn't there?"

"Still is," Bob answered. "The bank holds it. It's only for a couple of thousand. But with these last two bad summers, two's as good as ten."

Jim considered this. "And my dad?" he asked. "Did he ever get out from under?"

The lawman shook his head. "Far as I know, Davies is still carrying him along."

"Davies?" Jim echoed sharply.

"Didn't you know? The bank nearly went on the rocks last summer. Mark Davies tossed in forty thousand and took it over."

"So?" This was all adding up, was making more sense to Jim now.

As though reading his friend's thoughts, Rand nodded. "I know. I've thought the same thing. If Davies ever takes those two outfits, he's got the whole Willow Creek Basin."

He looked up at Jim in a speculative way and abruptly rose from the chair, stepping over to the big door set in the middle of the rear wall. There he took down a brass key from a nail on the door facing, saying as he opened the big lock: "Got something here to show you. And you're not going to like it."

Swinging the heavy door open, he motioned to Jim to follow and stepped through.

A momentary wariness struck through Jim, then left him feeling a little foolish. Here was a friend he could trust, trust all the way. He went into the jail to find Bob standing in the narrow corridor facing the bars of two cells, looking down into the left-hand one at a figure sprawled on the cot there.

This was a semidark and smelly place, the only source of light and air being a small barred skylight. The light was so poor that it was several moments before Jim could make out the features of the man on the cot and recognize Tate Higgins. Outside the wind dropped briefly and he could hear Tate's even breathing.

"Still pulling at the bottle, eh?" Jim drawled, a smile on his lean face.

"Still," Rand agreed gravely, "only finally it's cost someone. Your dad."

Jim shrugged. "It's cost the old man in a lot of ways. Keeping Tate out of trouble these last ten years. What is it this time?"

"Day before yesterday, Tate came in for a load of grub. Had a few drinks at the Pride and left town along about dark. He must've bought a bottle and killed it on the way home."

"The usual," Jim said.

"Anyway, your dad finally got tired of waiting for him and turned in. Along about midnight the horses in that small corral started raising hell and woke him. He found his barn on fire and Tate staggering around near the well, trying to draw water to put it out. Naturally Tate doesn't remember how it happened."

"He never could remember when he'd been drinking," Jim said as the full impact of what Rand had been telling him struck home. "How bad was it?" he asked soberly.

"The barn's gone along with some machinery. A couple of horses had to be shot."

Jim turned and went out. He heard Rand closing the jail door behind him. When he finally faced the sheriff again, the flat planes of his face were sharper and there was no longer that warmth in his blue eyes. "Anyone using that shack of Davies's up along Bear Ridge?" he asked.

"No. Why?"

"I'm going up there."

"To stay?"

Jim nodded.

He reached over and turned down the wick of the lamp that was smoking. "What'll it get you, Jim, if you stay around?"

"Who can tell? Nothing maybe. Then again. . . ."

"Why do it? If you're spotted and the word gets to Davies or Jeff Mears, they'll put that whole Block D crew out after you. And if they turn you over to me, there's not one thing I can do to help."

"I rode out on a thing like this once," Jim reminded him.

"There was nothing you could do about that rustling charge," Rand insisted. "You were framed. So you got out. There's nothing you can do about this. So the thing to do is ride."

Jim gave a slow shake of the head. "I'll look around."

"Look where?"

Jim's only answer to that was a shrug. He moved the chair from the door, letting it blow open. He didn't look back as he went out.

II

In those two hours since leaving town that same restless energy and impatience of the past week had been in Jim Roday. But now at sundown, as he climbed the long slope below the Halletts' log house, he felt played out, weary to the bone, without hope. His brief visit with his father had added nothing to what he already knew. Except for one thing. John Roday no longer had faith in his son, although he'd tried not to show it.

Jim swung wearily out of the saddle at the pole fence footing the Hallett yard, tied the sorrel alongside the gate, and walked on through. The light was too poor for him to recognize immediately the figure that came up out of the chair on the wide porch.

It wasn't until that figure called sharply—"Sis! Come out here."—that he knew who it was.

He had stopped at the foot of the steps and was staring up at Bill Hallett before Bill spoke again, this time tartly. "Either I'm seein' things or. . . ." He broke off momentarily, before adding loudly and urgently: "Mary! It's Jim Roday."

Jim heard a light step crossing the darkened room beyond the open door as he said quietly: "Can I come up, Bill?"

"Don't know whether you can or not," Bill Hallett said levelly as they eyed each other.

Jim was unsurprised by Bill's antagonism. His attention shifted abruptly as Mary Hallett came out of the door. She stopped just clear of the opening and what little he could see of her showed him a tall pretty girl whose dark eyes even in this poor light were bright with loathing and hatred.

"Get out," she said so softly that he could barely hear her. "Get out or I swear I'll turn a gun on you."

"Easy, Sis, easy," Bill said. His glance held to Jim. "What's on your mind?"

Jim had no chance to reply, for Mary spoke again. "Get rid of him," she said, her voice breaking with anger. "And don't ever ride this way again, Jim Roday. I'll shoot you on sight."

"Now look, Mary . . . ," Bill began.

But she cut him off, swinging around into the door. "Do you get rid of him or do I?"

"But this is. . . ."

"Forget it," Jim put in.

All at once he saw the futility of any compromise between them. He turned away and went down along the path and through the gate.

He was gathering up the reins when he heard a step behind him and swung around to find Bill Hallett coming through the gate.

From the porch, Mary called: "Bill, come back here!"

Bill muttered an oath and came up to Jim. "You were never a fool," he said. "And if all they've tallied against you was true, this'd be a damn' fool play. What's on your mind?"

Jim chose his words carefully, knowing how much they had to count.

"A lot of things," he answered finally. "I came here knowing I was wanted. Only that. Today Bob told me I bushwhacked your dad. Maybe I've been doing a lot of things like that I don't know about. You know of anything else?"

Hallett considered this and for a moment his expression lost its challenging enmity. But then his face tightened once more. "You've developed the habit of talking smooth, fella."

For a moment a live burning anger flared in Jim. Then wordlessly he swung up into the saddle.

"All right, I take that back," Bill said sharply. "But we've been hating you too damn' long to have flowers ready and waiting."

"It's no good," Jim told him. "I'll drag along on my own."

"You're staying in this country?"

Jim nodded. "For a while. To see what I can run onto."

"Where you staying?"

Jim's first instinct was to give an indefinite answer. But all at once he realized that placing trust in Bill Hallett might be one way of overcoming the man's hostility.

So he said: "In that line shack on Bear Ridge."

Bill frowned. "The rats have taken it over."

"I'll clean it up." Jim was about to turn the sorrel out from the gate when he thought of something. "Did you see that sign over on the ridge after they got Hugh?" he asked.

"No. Bob had a look at it before it washed out. We had a storm that day. It rained during the funeral."

Hallett gave this information in a flat uncompromising tone.

"No one else saw it then?"

Hallett shrugged. "I don't think so. But I can ask Mary. She sees Bob now and then. More than I do. She'd know."

Jim nodded. All he said was—"See you later."—and rode away.

The better part of an hour later he discovered that Bill Hallett had been right about the pack rats. The roof of the shack was half gone and the inside littered with straw and shreds of cloth torn from the single bunk's thin mattress. Jim had heard the rats scurrying away as he forced the sprung door open, and now, having surveyed it in the light of a match, he knew that he would spend a more comfortable night outside.

A hundred yards back through the pines south of the shack

he found a small grassy clearing. There he off-saddled and staked out the sorrel and made his bed behind an outcrop of rock. Hunger was gnawing at him and he built his fire and cooked his meal quickly, wolfing the food. Then he hit the blankets, aching with weariness.

The brittle explosion of a rifle shot brought Jim suddenly awake. He sat up in his blankets as the high whine of a ricocheting bullet cut the stillness of the cold, before-dawn air. A second shot cracked out from the crest of a rise close above, then another and another, evenly spaced, deliberate.

He lifted the blankets aside and pulled on his boots, counting now—four—five—six—seven. Abruptly the shots stopped. He reached over and drew his .30-30 from its scabbard and was coming erect when the rifle began speaking again in that same methodical way. Once a rock-glancing bullet sang out over the deep void beyond the ridge. Facing the sound of the rifle, Jim stared up through the trees, trying to pick out details in the gray half light.

The rifle went silent a second time and the stillness settled down once more. Then the faint clatter of an iron-shod hoof striking rock sounded from above. Jim listened for that sound again. But it didn't come.

Taking the carbine, he made a wide circle and climbed the rise. When he finally stood on its summit, the light was stronger and he could look down on the shack, less than a hundred yards away, and see it in minute detail. Even from here the weathered slabs showed their fresh scars, ripped and split by the bullets.

The gravelly earth up here told Jim little. But farther down along the far side he came upon the tracks of a horse. The line of the sign swung northward about a quarter mile back from the ridge and, standing there, his glance going in that direction, he remembered meeting a stranger riding a Block D branded horse on the timbered trail to his father's layout yesterday afternoon.

"So it's Davies again," he breathed, the anger crowding him.

He was sure of it. Sure even though he remembered that Bob Rand, Bill Hallett, and probably Mary knew of his intention to come up here. Rand he trusted and immediately put aside as a possibility. Bill Hallett probably hated him enough to try to kill him, but Bill would choose a more direct way, would meet him openly in an even shoot-out. Mary seemingly despised him even more than her brother, but this shooting had been a cold, deliberate, sure thing and no woman could have done it.

No. Mark Davies was the answer. It tied in with everything else that had gone on in Jim's absence. The rider he had met yesterday would naturally have been curious over the presence of a stranger in the basin. He'd have gone back to Block D and reported either to Davies or Jeff Mears and described Jim. They had probably sent someone—possibly Jeff Mears himself—to watch the Hallett layout and seen Jim ride in, followed him from the Hallett place, and then on up here.

He could be thankful now for having arrived here after dark, for the luck that sent him from the shack back into the timber where his supper fire had been hidden. But that thankfulness was a short-lived emotion before his anger, an emotion that slowly took complete possession of him.

The temptation to go down and examine the shack more closely was strong. But he forced himself to a wariness that made him roll his blankets, saddle, and ride a full mile deeper into the timber before building his breakfast fire in the shelter of a high-walled, narrow cañon.

When his hunger was satisfied, Jim mounted the sorrel and struck north into the higher hills, anger still strong in him but now blended with a cool cunning.

Twice he came upon trails, pausing each time to dismount and ground-halter the gelding while he went ahead to scan the worn earth. He found no fresh sign. But this didn't disappoint him, sure as he was of the answer.

Mark Davies's Block D sprawled outward from both banks of Willow Creek where the timber had been gouged out at the head of the high basin. It was typical of the man, Jim thought as he sighted the layout through the wind-swaying pines, that in building his place Davies hadn't wasted one square foot of the grass lower down. The house, shaped like a squared-off C facing south, was built of logs and served as owner's quarters, bunkhouse, and cook shack.

Jim remembered that Davies lived in the three small rooms of the far western wing. And now, as he saw that the timber crowded that portion of the building, he could smile. He made a mile-wide circle to come down through the trees there and left the sorrel a good two hundred yards above.

He gained the shelter of a low-growing cedar close behind the house and stood there a moment. Directly opposite the cedar was a dusty-paned window half open at the bottom. Looking both ways quickly and seeing no one, Jim crossed the last twenty feet to the house.

A glance in under the raised window showed him a bedroom. No one was in it. Lifting the window as far as it would go, he climbed in.

The bedroom was plain, a bed, a straight chair, a chest of drawers, and a curtained wardrobe along the far wall the only furnishings. Across the chair lay a pair of scarred chaps. A mound of soiled clothing lay in the corner nearest the window.

From beyond the closed door a deep voice boomed out plainly enough for Jim to hear the words: "Jeff, get in here."

It was Mark Davies who had spoken. His arrogant tone now lifted the pitch of Jim's anger to the point where he crossed the room and threw the door open. He was looking out into the hallway on the far side of which another door stood open. He crossed the hallway, went through that door.

The burly shape of Block D's owner stood at the single window of the room, his office. His back was to the door.

He said sourly, without turning: "Who the devil would be shootin' deer up there this time of year? Think up a better one."

Jim had time to survey the room carefully, knowing that Davies had heard him come in and supposed it was Jeff Mears. Half a dozen carbines and a shotgun leaned against the end of a horsehair sofa that took up most of the space of one side wall, facing a flat-topped desk along the other. A row of *Stockmen's Gazette* issues filled a shelf above the sofa. There were three chairs, a cushioned one at the desk. Slickers, a hat, a rope, and a sheepskin coat hung from pegs alongside the door.

One pane was gone from the window's upper sash and now, as a wind gust traveled the yard, the blind at the window flapped noisily.

That sound seemed to try Davies's patience, for he spoke querulously: "I said think up a better one." He swung around, scowling heavily.

His full square face went slack when he saw who it was. Jim reached back and pushed the door shut with the toe of a boot.

Davies's glance shifted momentarily to the end of the sofa and the guns standing there, before it whipped back again.

"Go on. Make a try," Jim drawled.

The rancher's surprise had faded. He opened his mouth to speak, thought better of it, and closed it again.

"Go ahead. Try and collect your thousand," Jim taunted. "Your hardcase messed up that job on the ridge this morning. Maybe you'll have better luck yourself."

"What hardcase?" Davies said finally. "You mean those shots up on Bear Ridge along about sunup?"

"You wouldn't know, would you?" When Jim got no reply, but only what he judged was a feigned look of perplexity, he went on: "Just like not knowing who fired the barn down at our place the other night and wished the job on Tate."

"You're damn' right I don't know about that," Davies stated flatly.

"And you didn't pay one of your killers to blow a hole through Hallett. And you're not one damned bit interested in closing out on those two outfits so your fence'll take in the rest of the basin." Jim laughed mirthlessly. "It goes as far back as three years, doesn't it? When you framed me with that rustling."

Out in the hall a board squeaked. Jim tensed as he caught the sound, but then relaxed as the wind flapped the blind at a window.

"You're puffin' names to me no man's ever dared to, Roday," Davies said soberly.

"I've only started, mister."

"In the first place," the rancher went on, making a visible effort to control his anger, "I don't even hold the paper on Halletts' and your father's place any longer. The bank sold them to a Denver man over two months ago."

"Sure. You'd cover your tracks," Jim drawled. "That's all part of. . . ."

He broke off as he caught a hint of motion. He wheeled, right hand streaking up and palming out the Colt. A numbing blow chopped his wrist down, sent the gun spinning across the floor, and Jeff Mears's hard shoulder slam knocked him off balance and staggering back into the desk.

Braced against the desk, Jim lifted a boot and met the foreman's rush, throwing all his weight into straightening his leg and prodding back the brawny Mears. Off to his left, Davies moved in at him and wheeled out from the desk, sweeping a china lamp from its corner, half throwing it at the man. As the lamp crashed to the floor, he turned and swung as Mears rushed him again, missing with his right, and his left connecting with the other man's shoulder. Mears kicked out and raked Jim's shin with a sharp-rowelled spur. Jim suddenly closed on him, spinning him around and lifting him bodily from the floor.

Holding Mears that way, he heaved sharply around and the foreman's legs caught Davies in the midriff and knocked him sideways onto the sofa. Jim suddenly let Mears go, bringing up a knee brutally in the small of the man's back as he fell. He saw Davies reaching for the guns at the sofa end and picked up the small chair standing by the door, swinging and throwing it. Davies bent double and the chair hit the wall above his head, coming apart.

Jim caught Mears as he was rising, caught him with a hard full right below the ear. Mears went down loosely, unconscious. Then a pair of arms closed on Jim from behind and a boot tripped him and he went down, a man's solid weight coming down on him to drive the wind from his lungs. He kicked out but could find no target. Breathing heavily, he lay there, arms still pinned.

"Let him up, Ed," he heard Davies say. The hold on his arms eased and the other's weight left his back, and, when he rolled over, it was to see the dour-looking hand he had met on the trail yesterday coming erect beside Davies at the desk.

The rancher held a gun he had taken from a desk drawer and with it motioned to Jim. "On your feet," he said.

Jim rose, still reaching for wind. Davies nodded to the rope on the wall peg and Ed stepped over there, took it down, and uncoiled it.

Davies thumbed back the .45's hammer. "I'm deliverin' you to the sheriff, Roday," he said. "It's up to you whether you go in dead or alive." With a meager lift of the gun, he motioned to his man.

Thirty seconds later Jim's arms were bound so tightly that all he could move was his hands. The Block D man left him then and knelt beside Jeff Mears. Davies had laid the .45 on the desk and was observing Jim narrowly.

"Just for the record, Roday," he said, "I know less than you about those shots on the ridge this mornin'."

"Save it for church," Jim drawled. That same unreasoning anger he had ridden in with was still holding him.

Ordinarily such a reply would have touched off the rancher's unstable temper but now, strangely, he seemed unruffled. "How long've you been around?" he queried.

"Long enough not to like the smell of things," Jim answered flatly.

Davies shrugged and turned away, saying to Ed: "We'll take him on in to Rand this afternoon. There's a directors' meetin' at five. No use my goin' in now and waitin' around the whole day."

III

Mark Davies and four Block D riders reached Pine City with their prisoner shortly before 5:00 that afternoon. No one was in the sheriff's office, so Davies unceremoniously opened the jail with the keys that always hung near the cell-block door. He put Jim in an empty cell.

The rancher stood in the narrow corridor a moment studying the sleeping Tate Higgins in the adjoining cell. Tate lay in almost the exact position as yesterday, breathing sonorously with his mouth open. Then, with a shrug, Davies went out, closing and locking the cell-block door.

The day had paid Jim no dividends beyond strengthening his conviction that Mark Davies's scheming brain was behind the developments of the past weeks. The shooting on the ridge this morning had at first been an enigma to him, remembering as he did Davies's remark before knowing that it was Jim, not Jeff Mears, in the room with him. On the surface those words had had the ring of innocence, of Davies's knowing nothing of who had fired those shots. But Jim had finally reasoned that in the reference to deer shooting he had caught the rancher and his foreman in an attempt at thinking up an explanation of the shots on the ridge—an explanation to offer anyone who had heard them and might become curious.

Davies's denials of knowing anything of Hallett's murder or of the burning of the Roday barn followed the pattern Jim had expected. The sale of the mortgages by the bank was, he admitted, a clever piece of maneuvering. But here again was added proof of Davies's cunning.

By the time they had started the ride for town, Jim had become convinced of one thing—that, when this was over, not one particle of evidence would point to Mark Davies beyond the final outcome of his having possession of the two basin outfits. This morning, the Block D owner had missed his chance at killing the only man who had ever fought him. Now he was leaving it to the law to deal with Jim.

Jim listened as Davies's heavy step crossed the office. He caught the thud of the street door slamming and, frowning as he breathed the stale air of this close room, turned from the barred head of the cell and stepped over to look down at Tate Higgins.

He saw Tate's eyes open all at once and peer up at him. The next moment the oldster was whispering: "Is he gone?"

Jim nodded over his surprise, and then Tate swung his feet to the floor and stood up. His eyes were clear and alert. He smiled broadly, exposing a gap where two teeth were missing. "Damn. It's good to see you, Jim," he said, and thrust a hand through the bars.

Jim took the proffered hand. "Playing 'possum, eh?"

Tate nodded, fingering his drooping gray mustache. "Have been for three days." He squinted one eye. "Take a look." He turned and lifted aside the straw mattress on his cot. Underneath it lay two full quart bottles of whiskey.

Not understanding, Jim said: "You haven't touched 'em?"

"Not a drop," Tate told him with excusable pride. His glance went up to the barred opening. "Someone . . . damned if I know who . . . has been passing me a bottle through the skylight every night since I been here. I killed the first one, three nights ago. Then I got to thinking."

As the oldster paused, Jim finished the thought for him: "That someone's interested in keeping you under the influence?"

Tate grinned toothily, nodded. Then an expression of contriteness patterned his gaunt face. "Jim," he said, "I've got one hell of a lot to make up to you and the old man."

Jim lifted his shoulders a little. "You've got a taste for the stuff. They say you can't do much about it when it's that way."

Tate shook his head almost savagely. "I ain't talking about that. Sure, I like my red-eye. But it's something else."

Jim waited, wondering what the other was getting at.

"Remember Ike Stallings?" Tate asked.

"That's a damned fool question," Jim drawled.

Tate lifted a hand. "All right. Don't get sore now. I had to start some way." He swallowed as though his mouth was dry. "How it got out that Ike had bought that rustled beef of Hallett's from you, I'll never know. One day I'll see him and get the truth. Anyway, here's how it goes. Remember the time I asked your old man to hold back my wages? Except tobacco money?"

Jim nodded. "Thought you'd cure yourself of the habit if you couldn't buy the stuff."

"Yeah. Well, it'll sound funny to you now, but I got sore as hell at John for that. Even though it was my own idea. Then one Saturday night here in town I run into Ike."

Jim's brows came up and the oldster noticed that and said: "Oh, he used to ride over whenever he wanted. Not many around here knew him. Anyway, that night I borrowed twenty dollars from him and got drunk. Something I never told you was that Ike and me worked for the same outfit before I hired on with John. Well, after that night I stayed sober a long time, couple of months. Then one day hauling salt up to that upper tank I run onto Ike again. He didn't want his money back. Only asked if I'd like to make some extra, the easy way."

"Rustling?" queried Jim.

"Rustling," Tate admitted. "In the old days Ike and me were . . . well, you might say partners. Until I got the hell scared out of me. After that I went straight. But this time, the way Ike explained it, it seemed easy."

He paused, turned and took a bottle from under his mattress. Uncorking it, he offered it to Jim. When Jim shook his head, Tate said simply—"I'm going to need this."—and took a long swallow out of the bottle.

He returned the bottle to its place under the mattress. "So three nights later I made up a story. Told John I wanted the next day off to go to a dance over in Paiute. That night I rode 'way up in the hills and picked up the first twenty or thirty critters I come across. They just happened to be Hallett's stuff. I drove 'em over Windy Pass. By noon the next day I was holding 'em in a cañon Ike had told me about. He met me there, paid me fifty dollars, and said to forget the loan. The whole thing was easy. Damned if I wouldn't have done it again if they hadn't framed it on you."

Beads of perspiration were standing out on the oldster's brow now. He looked up at Jim, saw the cold impassive set of his face, and went on stubbornly: "So it was me that framed you, Jim. I'd have owned up to it except that. . . ." A sudden half-angry glint came to his eye. "Damn it, Jim! I'm crooked. Always have been."

The anger that was in Jim melted before this admission. And as he looked beyond the facts Tate had given him, a strange thought came to him.

"Maybe it was best the way it happened," he said. "Maybe if he hadn't gotten away with it that first time, he'd have given up and we'd never have known who he was."

"You mean Ike?"

Jim shook his head. "No. I mean whoever paid Ike to have you steal that beef."

"Davies?"

"It looks like it."

"Sure as hell does," Tate agreed. He was relieved now. "He figured you'd be the only one to put up a fight when he made his grab for those two outfits. Got rid of you."

Jim was thinking of something else. "How about the other night, Tate?" he asked. "The night you burned the barn down?"

"Me?" Tate soberly shook his head. "Jim, I'll swear to my dying day it wasn't me. Even if I don't remember." He squinted, eying Jim directly. "Now there's another funny thing. Here's someone been passing me whiskey every night. That night, the night of the fire, it was the same. I'd had some drinks before I picked up that load from the store. But I wasn't near drunk. Then, when I come out of the store, I found a bottle under the seat cushion."

"And you drank it?"

"Sure. Who wouldn't? It was part gone and I figured some jasper a little too much under the weather had put it there by mistake, thinking it was his rig."

"Then you were tanked when you got home?"

Tate didn't answer at once, frowning and scratching his head. Finally he drew a deep sigh. "I've been trying to remember, Jim. All I know is. . . ."

They heard the office door slam and someone crossed the room there. Tate's look became panicked until Jim said softly: "Hit the blankets again. You haven't been awake."

Tate lay down immediately and at once appeared to be dead asleep, snoring a little. As the key rattled in the door's big lock, Jim sat on his cot, back to the end wall, boots on the straw-filled mattress. He pulled his hat down over his eyes.

When Bob Rand swung the door open and stepped in, Jim gave a start, sat up, and stretched and yawned.

Rand closed the door and, with a brief glance at Tate, came over to Jim's cell. His expression was grave and for a moment he met the straightforward glance of Jim's blue eyes with a look almost of sadness. Then, letting his breath out, he drawled: "Well, you've done it."

Jim nodded.

Rand went on with a touch of anger: "Last night I lay awake planning things. How you and me between us could dope this out." He shrugged wearily. "Now you're here. Not doing anyone any damned good. Not even yourself."

"Bob, someone made a try for me up at that shack this morning. I don't take that from any man."

"When you're playing for stakes like this, you take a lot of things," Rand told him. "Any ideas on who made the try at you?"

"Not one. Except . . . the hunch I played that it was Davies. I was damned near loco this morning," Jim said gravely. "Didn't think, I guess."

Rand waved a hand impatiently. "If you know it, let's forget it. How did you make out with Bill and Mary? Or did you see them?"

Jim nodded. "I did. They were what you might call unfriendly."

"Bill wouldn't listen to you?"

"He might've if it hadn't been for Mary. I just wasted my time."

Rand was silent a moment before saying: "Then that leaves you without anyone to count on. Except me. How about your father?"

Jim only shook his head.

"Don't you see the spot you've put me in?" Rand asked irritably. "I'm sheriff here. You're wanted. Any personal feelings I have can't count for a damn now."

"I know."

Again the lawman gave that meager lift of the shoulders. "Well, I'll try and think of something," he said. He stepped over to the adjoining cell. "Might as well get rid of this problem right now." He unlocked the door and went in and reached down to shake Tate.

The oldster only grunted and turned over. But Rand kept on and in the next half minute Tate made the pretence of coming reluctantly awake, and staggered to his feet.

Rand shook the old man harder now that he had him standing. "Tate, I'm sending you home," he said. "Now for Pete's sake stay away from the bottle for a while."

"Shur, Bob," Tate mumbled. "Stay 'way from the stuff f'r the resta m'life."

Rand led him out, leaving the jail door open. Jim heard them go out onto the street and out there Rand asked: "You sure you can ride?" Tate made some incoherent reply, and then there was silence for a time. Finally Rand reappeared for a moment, telling Jim: "I'll go over to Joe's and get your supper."

It was ten minutes before the sheriff was back with a pail full of stew and half a loaf of bread and a lantern. He opened the cell and passed the things in to Jim. "Nothing fancy," he said. "Need anything more?"

"No. This'll do." Jim hung the lantern above the cot and Bob closed and locked the door.

Jim ate only part of the meal, although it was good. He had no appetite. He couldn't even think straight. He was thankful, shortly, to find that he was sleepy. He blew out the lantern and pulled up a blanket and tried to keep from thinking he was beaten.

IV

Jim came sluggishly awake, lying for a moment in a confused groping to know where he was. The stale air seemed to have drugged him and he pushed up onto one elbow and shook his head, slowly remembering.

A glance at the skylight showed him the pale blur of stars, too indistinct to recognize so that he could gauge the time. He wondered what had wakened him and had his answer as the lock on the jail door faintly clicked. Instantly his nerves went tight and he threw back the blanket and rolled full length to the floor, remembering clearly the shots on the ridge.

The hinges of the door creaked suddenly with a noise that raised the hackles along his neck. They squealed again, more faintly, and he knew the door had closed. Listening intently, Jim thought he could hear a man's breathing. Someone was in the room with him.

Suddenly a slit of light from a shaded lantern cut the blackness of his cell, swinging to and fro and settling finally fully on him.

"What's the matter?" a voice asked. "The bed too hard?"

Jim lay there rigid, waiting for Bill Hallett's next move. He was searching the shadows, trying to make out the other's shape, trying to catch the glint of light from a gun barrel. But the lantern's bright slit blinded him.

In another moment he passed beyond fear and into that mood of recklessness and not caring that always came to him in times of acute danger. He picked himself up, drawling: "Get it over with."

"Get what over with?" Hallett asked. He set the lantern on the floor then and moved around it to the cell door. There came the jingle of keys as he added: "You're leaving here, fella. We've smoked the pipe of peace."

This was the Bill Hallett Jim remembered, and, as the tension fell away, he found that he was trembling slightly, that hope had come alive in him once more.

"That sister of yours'll take the hide off you for this, Bill," he said.

"She's been rawhiding me all day." The door swung open. "Only not the way you think. Last night she pried it out of me where you were staying. Then this morning she was up and out before I was awake. She heard shots as she was coming up to the ridge and she saw how the shack had been beaten up. Came back down and carried on like a crazy woman. She was sure you'd been killed and your carcass dragged away."

"That should've made her happy."

"Well, it didn't. Damned if I know how she thought it out. But she did. Said she knew you were in trouble and that we were the only ones who could help. Made me ride over to Davies's with her and sit there in the timber watching the place and waiting for something to happen. Finally it did. We saw them bring you in."

For the first time in over a week Jim Roday felt the surge of an emotion that was akin to happiness. It lifted him immediately from the deep depression of the past two days.

Bill picked up the lantern, waited for Jim to come out of the cell. "Mary's hell on wheels when she gets started," he drawled. "Went down to the livery a few minutes and helped herself to one of Bob's saddles and that big black of Doc Erlanger's. Next thing I know, they'll have her for horse stealing. And these keys.

She knew where Bob had 'em."

Mary was holding the three horses in the alley behind the jail, out of the wind. As Jim appeared and stood before her, she looked up at him a moment with a sober expression, and then held out her hand to him.

"Can an old friend say she's sorry, Jim?" she asked.

"She can," Jim answered, and the strong pressure of her grasp told him even more of the change in her than her words.

"What now?" Bill asked, breaking an awkward silence.

"That's up to Jim," Mary said. She stepped in beside a wiry white-stockinged mare, the smallest of the three horses, and unbuckled a saddle pouch and took something from it. Handing it to Jim, she told him: "This was Dad's. He'd want you to have it if he were here now."

In the starlight, Jim looked down on a simply tooled shell belt and holster. The gun was horn-handled, a .38 Colt. He knew it now, remembered Hugh Hallett's pride in this weapon. Here was as final and convincing a sign of Mary Hallett's changed belief in him as anything could be. Soberly he buckled the filled belt about his waist and thonged the holster to his thigh.

"Tate Higgins got started on a tale today that'll interest you two," he said. "Didn't get a chance to finish telling me what it was. Bob let him go tonight. Suppose we head for our place and hear the rest of it."

They turned down the alleyway beyond the barn and then rode out the wind-swept street of the sleeping town, heads down against the fitful blasts. They were barely past the house when Mary began her questions. Bill, riding ahead, was impatient and once called back for them to hurry. Then he heard their talk and dropped back to listen as Jim explained in detail all that had gone on these past two days.

Finally Jim had finished and they fell silent, covering several miles without a further word. Then Mary said abruptly: "You shouldn't have let us run you out three years ago."

"I know."

"If I'd only believed then as I wanted to," she said, letting him read his own meaning into her words.

Above Rocky Point, where the trail narrowed and cut up the high-angling face of the rim that footed Willow Basin, they came upon it. Bill, riding ahead, pulled in sharply, calling back: "Hang it, a slide!"

They came up with him as he turned his horse up the steep slope, intending to ride around a heap of rubble and rock that blocked the trail. Jim, more curious, said: "Hold on." He was thinking back, trying to remember, looking up the slope that was indistinct and shadowed in the starlight.

"This was never a bad place," he said finally. "Farther up it is. But that rock up there is sound."

And now he looked downward, seeing that the rim dropped steeply away from the trail for thirty feet or so to a jutting ledge. Below that ledge was a like downward distance to the rim's base where it joined the flats.

Directly downward a section of the ledge was broken off, giving the rim face at this point a straight downward angling line to a mound of rubble at its base.

Bill had turned and come back and was following the direction of Jim's glance. "Something went over here, hit that ledge, and caved it in," he said. "Must've shaken loose that stuff from above."

"Could it have been a wagon?" Mary asked.

Jim swung down out of his saddle. "How about your rope, Bill?" he drawled.

He took the rope Bill handed him, tying it to the horn of Erlanger's black gelding. Mary saw what he intended and came aground to hold the reins of the black as he tossed the coil of rope out and watched it uncurl downward. He ignored Bill's puzzled—"I don't get it."—and stepped over the trail's edge and downward, braced erect by his hold on the rope.

Along part of that downward distance he lost all footing and lowered himself by taking his full weight against the rope. Once the wind caught him as he hung free and pushed him sharply against the face of the rim. Finally his boots felt the outward slope of the slide and he let the rope go and half slid, half walked the remaining distance to the mound's downward margin.

Now that he was down here, he was thinking that there was little this heap of dirt and rock could tell him. Angling around its base and finding nothing, he began to climb the far margin back to the rope. Then a dark scar against the pale shadow of the slide surface off to his left caught his attention and took him over there on hands and knees.

He stopped, crouching, within arm's reach of what he had seen, sudden shock settling through him. A boot and a man's lower leg were cocked up at an awkward angle out of the rubble.

V

Two minutes later, after frantically digging into the rubble, Jim settled back on his heels. He said softly: "Here's hoping the drinks are on the house from now on, old-timer." And he had his deep regret over the price Tate Higgins had paid for his part in this.

He thought then of finishing the digging out of the body and taking it on into town tonight. But time now was a precious thing and in the end he climbed on up the slope, knowing that were Tate alive he would have understood. Holding the rope once more, he worked his way over to a point above the body. There he loosed a slide of rubble by kicking loose a holding rock. When the wind had whipped the gray fog of dust away, the body was no longer there. Tate was safe until morning. And with that thought Jim climbed the face of the rim.

As he pulled himself back onto the trail, Bill said impatiently: "No luck?" When Jim didn't immediately answer, he added: "Time's wasting, friend. Let's get out and see Tate."

Jim nodded downward. "You won't have to ride far."

Mary caught her breath and Bill spoke quickly. "Down there?"

"Dead," Jim said. "Shot through the head."

For a long moment the two were wordless, taking in what he had told them. It was Mary who broke the silence. "Poor Tate. He was always making a new start."

Bill nodded soberly. He took out tobacco and rolled a smoke and passed the makings on over to Jim.

"Any ideas on who did it?" he asked

"No. But we might try and find out."

"How?" Mary asked.

Jim thought a moment, looking up at the stars. "It's not too late," he said. "The night owls would still be hanging out at the Pride. And you'd have to tell Bob. Getting the word around might do some good before the night's over."

"What good?"

"Maybe a lot. If we made it the right kind of a story."

"The right kind?"

Jim nodded. "Suppose we say you and Mary found Tate just knocked out. Suppose he had come to long enough to tell you he saw who shot him, without naming who it was. You'd tell 'em that you and Mary had taken him over to your place and put him in that end room of your father's. You're in town after Doc Erlanger."

When Bill frowned, Mary said eagerly: "Whoever shot Tate might hear about it. He'd have to do something."

"But if it was Davies, he wouldn't get the word tonight," objected Bill.

"Yes, he would," Mary told him. "His horse was in the stable when I was there a while ago. That means he's probably staying over night at the hotel."

With a doubtful look still on his face, Bill stepped to his horse and climbed into the saddle. He said: "See you later at our place. Erlanger's going to be sore as hell at me making him ride all that way for nothing." He had lifted the reins, about to ride away, when he thought of something. "I'll tell Bob what really did happen."

"No," Jim said. "There's plenty of time for that. He's a poor liar. So tell him what you do the others."

Bill shook his head in perplexity and turned his horse back toward Pine City.

The wind quickly cut off the sound of his going. Mary looked up at Jim. "You know, don't you?" she said evenly. At Jim's answering shrug, she insisted: "Could you tell me?"

"Not yet. I might be wrong."

Mary turned to her horse then and they rode up and around the block in the trail, the black once slipping dangerously but steadying as Jim pulled his head up.

About forty minutes later they raised a single light that was the Hallett place high along the timber-edged basin. Here the wind was a wild thing, shrieking through the pines with a never-ending cry. Jim sent Mary up to the house and took the horses to the corral.

When he joined her in the kitchen, taking the cup of coffee she had waiting for him, he nodded to the door that led to the main part of the log house. "We'd better get things fixed."

Mary gave him a puzzled look as he led the way in across the living room that was chinked with white plaster. He took the lamp from the big center table and headed for a door on the far side.

As he was opening it, Mary said: "I haven't been in there, Jim. Not since that night."

Jim paused. "Then let me do it," he said, going on into Hugh Hallett's bedroom.

It was a simply furnished large cubicle, its severity relieved by a feminine touch—printed calico curtains at the single window, an embroidered white scarf on the dresser. A wide bed, the dresser, two chairs, and a high mahogany wardrobe were ranged along the walls.

Jim turned down the spread on the bed, rumpled the pillow. In the wardrobe he found two blankets that he rolled and thrust under the bed covering. He stepped to the window and surveyed the bed, going back to it once to put a bend in the roll of blankets. Finally it satisfied him. He left the lighted lamp on the dresser and went back into the living room.

"I might need a rifle," he said.

Mary went to the gun rack in the back corner and came back carrying a .30-30. She handed him a box of shells, looking up at him in a questioning way but saying nothing.

"You'd better turn in," he told her. He saw a canvas Windbreaker of Bill's lying on the couch and stepped over to pull it on, grinning as he extended his arms and forced them far out of the too-short sleeves. "Just right."

Mary smiled faintly but was in no mood for light-heartedness. "You're really expecting someone?" she asked.

He nodded and, the rifle under his arm, turned to the door.

She said quickly—"Jim."—and he stopped.

She came over to him and what he saw in her eyes stirred him first to disbelief, then wonder and a sense of something new and with deep meaning lying in this moment.

"Be careful, Jim," was all she said as she turned away. But there was an eloquence to those words that was not lost upon him.

Jim went out into the night and around the far corner of the house, leaning into the quick rush of the wind there. He passed the lighted window of Hugh Hallett's bedroom and looked out and across the yard beyond, finally heading for the vague low outline of the root cellar and the tangle of willow alongside it where the spring came down the gradual slope beyond the edge of timber, about a hundred yards away. He loaded the carbine and put the box of shells in a jacket pocket.

VI

Jim hunkered down between the thicket's edge and the earth wall of the cellar, not making himself too comfortable, knowing he might have a long wait. His view of the bedroom window and the shaft of light beyond it was from time to time criss-crossed by the leafy pattern of willow branches swayed by the wind. He leaned the rifle against the wall beside him.

That look Mary had given him kept coming back and with it a dozen incidents he had filed far back in the pigeonholes of his mind. He remembered his first dance, how Mary had asked to be taken and how he had refused, and then finally his jealousy when she had come with another young fellow whose name he had forgotten. He thought of Bob Rand and began to wonder if he had read the right meaning into Mary's glance. Bill's casual mention of Mary and Bob the other night had its obscure meaning and he couldn't overlook that. And now the bitter-learned resignation and denial of these past three years was in him, making him feel that Mary Hallett was not for him.

When he thought to look up at the stars, he was surprised at what they told him. He had been sitting here for better than an hour. He realized abruptly that he was cold and stiff and that the restless pitch of the wind was pulling at his nerves. He stood up, his knee joints stiff, and looked into the far shadows of the yard, impatient because they told him nothing.

Something hard jabbed into his back and Bob Rand's voice said lazily, close behind him: "Don't move."

Jim wheeled halfway around in his surprise before reading the full meaning of his danger into the coolness of those words. He felt the weight of the .38 abruptly leave his thigh and then he made out the other's thin shape, taking a backward step.

Rand gave a low laugh. "The wind let you down. It would've been a good idea except for that."

Jim turned completely around now, the toe of his boot touching something stiffly yielding. It was the Winchester and his pulse quickened as he realized that his body had shielded the weapon from Rand's view.

"You took your time getting here," he said. "But you had to come, eh?"

Again Bob's low laugh rose above the sigh of the wind. "Bill lied about Tate. I'd found the jail empty. Putting two and two together, I knew it was you. You trumped up a good story."

Jim said nothing, waiting, his down-hanging right hand against the cold steel of the Winchester's barrel.

"Tate was dead when he fell out of his saddle," Rand said. "At fifty yards I couldn't miss."

The man's calm cold admission did more to bring home to Jim his danger than anything else. "So it all adds up," he drawled. "Ike Stallings, the sign in the timber no one else saw, the whiskey you passed in to Tate. Was Davies telling the truth when he said the bank had sold that paper to someone in Denver?"

He could see Rand well enough to catch his nod. "I have a brother in Denver. Asked him to make a small investment for me and keep his mouth shut," the sheriff admitted.

Jim leaned against the wall of the root cellar as Rand went on angrily: "I didn't want this, Jim. You asked for it. I gave you the chance to get out."

"And Mary," Jim asked. "What about her?"

Taking his chance on the depth of shadow, judging the lighted window behind him to be well out of line, Jim tilted the carbine up, shifted his hand suddenly, and gripped it lower along the fore part of the stock. He stiffened with apprehension when the butt of the weapon thudded against the wall. As the tempo of the wind in the timber above increased in pitch, he stood there expecting the slam of a bullet.

Then Rand said—"I'll marry her if she'll have me."—and Jim knew that the wind had played its second fateful part this night, hiding the sound from Rand.

"Would she, knowing this?" he asked tonelessly.

"Who said she'd know? This wind'll cover my tracks by morning. I'll borrow from the bank to buy back those two notes from this supposed stranger in Denver. When we're married, we'll live here."

"And let Davies take the blame?" Jim shifted his hold once more and now felt the trigger guard of the weapon right behind his hand.

"No one'll ever know about Davies, will they?" Amusement edged Rand's tone. "Maybe he's finished here. Maybe he'll never be able to live this down. Someone may have to take over his layout. The bank might go along with me after they buy Davies out."

A wind blast ripped through the crest of the pines close above, and in its covering sound Jim hefted the Winchester once more, caught it with his finger through the trigger guard. He thumbed back the hammer.

Its click rose audibly over the sudden dying sound of the wind and Jim saw Rand's frame stiffen. He lined the Winchester at his hip and squeezed the trigger and the sharp report came as the other lunged violently to one side. Rand's right hand was swinging up as Jim realized he hadn't hit him. Pushing out from the wall, he threw himself into the thicket, falling sideways. Rand's gun exploded deafeningly and the bullet broke a thick leafy stem and lashed it across Jim's cheek.

The branches cushioned Jim's fall. Lying there on his side, he swept aside the branches, levering in a new shell as the gun on the thicket's far side spoke again. His right shoulder jarred back from a hard impact. He aimed the Winchester a foot below the rosy wing of gun flame he had seen a moment ago through the branches. He squeezed the trigger and winced at the sharp pain the kick of the weapon sent through his shoulder. He levered again, shot again, and was only vaguely aware of a single answering explosion. Rolling out of the thicket, he lay there listening and, the wind dying now, heard Bob Rand cough.

That sound told him that one of his bullets had found a mark, for it was rattling cough of a man with congested lungs. Jim started crawling back along the wall of the root cellar, hugging the ground, left hand reaching out before him. Pain like the burning of a hot iron was in his right shoulder as he dragged the Winchester with that arm. He had covered about ten feet in this way when Rand shot blindly, the bullet tearing through the thicket. Hard on the heels of that shot came other sounds. First the faint but quickly strengthening hoof pound of running horses rising over the whine of the wind, coming along the trail below. And then Jim heard Mary's voice calling his name from close below.

All at once his groping hand touched something hard and cold and a moment later he was gripping Hugh Hallett's .38, knowing that Rand must have dropped it in his haste to dodge aside with that first shot. Jim let go the Winchester now, a deep thankfulness in him. Aiming a Colt blindly was hard enough, but lining a Winchester accurately without being able to see the front sight he had found infinitely harder. He crawled toward the back edge of the thicket where Rand waited, no longer minding the pain in his shoulder. And now he could hear two, or perhaps three riders running in toward the house. Shortly a man's voice shouted something down there. Although Jim couldn't be sure of that voice, it sounded a little like Mark Davies.

He was within a few feet of the thicket's back edge when Rand all at once spoke from close in front of him, spoke softly and hoarsely and in a labored breath: "I'm coming after you."

There was the scrape of a boot beyond the thicket and Jim realized that Rand was circling it on the far side. He stood up then and in two swift soundless strides was around the end of the thicket and seeing Rand's tall shape some thirty feet away between him and the lighted window below. Jim had his sure chance at the man. But from deep within him rose a perverse resolve not to use this advantage.

"Up here!" he called.

Rand whirled around, shooting as he moved. Jim felt the breath of a bullet along the side of his face. He thumbed a shot at Rand, then another, deliberately taking his time. He saw his second bullet jar Rand's tall frame backward. And now he deliberately raised the .38 and had a clear look at Rand's wide chest along the front sight as he squeezed the trigger. The bullet spun Rand halfway around and he went down loosely, the momentum of his fall carrying him over and onto his back, his arms spread-eagled.

A door slammed at the house, and, looking down there, Jim made out four figures, one of them Mary, by the flickering light of a lantern.

"Jim!" Bill Hallett's voice called stridently.

"Here," he answered, and they started up toward him. He was shaking a little now, feeling faint, and his shoulder throbbed with a steady aching. He moved his arm carefully and it was a relief to realize that no bones were broken. He sat down, laid the .38 on the ground beside him, and leaned over, resting his head on his knees, hearing them approach.

It was Mark Davies who spoke abruptly from close below, saying in an awed tone: "Great Tophet, it's Rand. Dead."

Jim lifted his head then and saw Davies holding the lantern, Doc Erlanger kneeling beside Rand's inert shape, and Bill and Mary coming toward him, several steps this side of Davies.

All at once Mary cried softly: "Jim, you're hurt."

Then Davies's voice sounded sharply. "Hold on, you two. Don't go near him." He suddenly reached down and snatched Rand's gun from the ground and lined it at Jim. "You, Roday!" he ordered. "Reach!"

Jim stayed as he was, right arm resting limply on the ground, bracing himself with his left, suddenly realizing something that had escaped him until this moment. He and he alone knew the enormity of Bob Rand's deception. No one, with the possible exception of Mary and Bill, would believe the things Rand had admitted. To all appearances, Rand had come out here on a hunch to arrest a prisoner who had broken jail, and had been killed doing his duty.

Bill and Mary had stopped at Davies's word and now Bill swung around on the man. "Easy, Davies," he drawled. "We'll hear what he has to say."

Davies's glance didn't stray from Jim. "What could he have to say?"

"You were talking to Bob before the shots came, Jim," Mary said urgently. And he saw that her eyes were pleading with him, bright with tears she couldn't hold back. All at once her look changed to one of defiance and she, too, turned toward Davies. "If Jim caught Bob Rand sneaking in on the house, it means that Bob killed Tate Higgins."

Davies smiled mirthlessly. "Why would he? No. He knew Roday was here and he came after him." He added ominously, his look still hard on Jim: "If you move that right hand, Roday, I'm going to let you have it."

"Mary," Jim said.

When she turned to him again, he told her: "Bob did kill Tate. And your father. He had his brother in Denver buy those notes from the bank under an assumed name."

"Think up a better one," Davies put in tauntingly.

"He even had the idea he could put all the blame on Davies and maybe in the end force Davies to pull out. Then he was going to buy up Davies's outfit," Jim went on, ignoring the interruption. "That's about all there was, Mary. He figured I knew he was the one and he came out after me."

"You'll need a damned good lawyer to sell that to a jury," Davies cut in once more. He added: "If you live long enough to stand trial."

"Try making a lynch mob out of your crew, Davies," Bill said angrily, "and I'll. . . ."

"Just a minute," Doc Erlanger's voice interrupted urgently.

They saw him bend close to the body on the ground and Jim realized that Rand wasn't dead. Jim pushed himself erect and a moment later he heard Rand speak weakly, the words indistinguishable.

The medico looked up quickly at Davies. "Did you hear that?"

Davies nodded, no longer looking at Jim. He went down on one knee beside the doctor. But Erlanger shook his head, saying simply: "Too late. He's gone."

Kneeling there, Davies looked across at Jim and said levelly: "I'm beggin' your pardon, Roday. What he said was . . . 'I'd have had that Block D layout, too. None of you could've stopped me. Why did Jim Roday have to come back here, anyway?' "

"Oh, Jim!" Mary cried, and came over to him. Then she was in his arms, her face uplifted. He kissed her tenderly, not minding the pain in his shoulder now.

He remembered something that made him say softly, so that the others couldn't hear: "Bill said something the other night about you and Bob."

Mary pushed away from him and looked up in a wondering way. "What about Bob and me?" She was silent a moment, finally understanding. "Never anyone but you, Jim," she said, coming close to him again. "It's been so long since you went away," she murmured. "So long trying not to believe in you but knowing there could never be anyone else."

All the restlessness and wildness and that sense of not belonging that had ridden so constantly with Jim Roday over these three years was gone now. He was home again.

ACKNOWLEDGMENTS

"Posse of Outlawed Men" first appeared in *Big-Book Western Magazine* (3-4/37). Copyright © 1937 by Popular Publications, Inc. Copyright © renewed 1965 by Dorothy S. Ewing. Copyright © 2010 by David S. Glidden for restored material.

"Rust Off a Tin Star" first appeared as "An Ex-Marshal Ramrods the *Malpaís*" in *Complete Western Book Magazine* (5/38). Copyright © 1938 by Newsstand Publications, Inc. Copyright © renewed 1966 by Dorothy S. Ewing. Copyright © 2010 by David S. Glidden for restored material.

"Nester Payoff" first appeared as "Hell-Born Hatred" in *Western Trails* (6/37). Copyright © 1937 by Magazine Publishers, Inc. Copyright © renewed 1965 by Dorothy S. Ewing. Copyright © 2010 by David S. Glidden for restored material.

"Amateur Gun Guard" first appeared in *Dime Western* (11/37). Copyright © 1937 by Popular Publications, Inc. Copyright © renewed 1965 by Dorothy S. Ewing. Copyright © 2010 by David S. Glidden for restored material.

"Dead Man's Assay" first appeared as "Dead Man's Draw" in *Fifteen Western Tales* (2/48). Copyright © 1948 by Popular Publications, Inc. Copyright © renewed 1976 by Dorothy S. Ewing. Copyright © 2010 by David S. Glidden for restored material.

"Willow Basin" first appeared as "Willow Basin Outcast" in *Western Story* (1/47). Copyright © 1947 by Street & Smith Publications, Inc. Copyright © renewed 1975 by Dorothy S.

ABOUT THE AUTHOR

Peter Dawson is the *nom de plume* used by Jonathan Hurff Glidden. He was born in Kewanee, Illinois, and was graduated from the University of Illinois with a degree in English literature. In his career as a Western writer he published sixteen Western novels and wrote over 120 Western short novels and short stories for the magazine market. From the beginning he was a dedicated craftsman who revised and polished his fiction until it shone as a fine gem. His Peter Dawson novels are noted for their adept plotting, interesting and well-developed characters, their authentically researched historical backgrounds, and his stylistic flair. During the Second World War, Glidden served with the U.S. Strategic and Tactical Air Force in the United Kingdom. Later in 1950 he served for a time as Assistant to Chief of Station in Germany. After the war, his novels were frequently serialized in *The Saturday Evening Post.* Peter Dawson titles such as *Royal Gorge* and *Ruler of the Range* are generally conceded to be among his best titles, although he was an extremely consistent writer, and virtually all his fiction has retained its classic stature among readers of all generations. One of Jon Glidden's finest techniques was his ability, after the fashion of Dickens and Tolstoy, to tell his stories via a series of dramatic vignettes which focus on a wide assortment of different characters, all tending to develop their own lives, situations, and predicaments, while at the same time propelling the general plot of the story toward a suspenseful conclusion. He was no less gifted as a master of the short novel and short story. *Dark Riders of Doom* (Five Star Westerns, 1996) was the first collection of his Western short novels and stories to be published. His next Five Star Western will be *Rider on the Buckskin.*